# TORPEDO STRIKE

*A WWII Action Thriller*

John Wingate

*Also in the WWII Action Thriller Series*

Never So Proud

Last Ditch

# TORPEDO STRIKE

Published by Sapere Books.

20 Windermere Drive, Leeds, England, LS17 7UZ,
United Kingdom

saperebooks.com



ISBN: 978-1-80055-341-5

ACKNOWLEDGEMENTS

I am greatly indebted to My Lords Commissioners of the Admiralty for their assistance, co-operation and permission to publish. In particular I wish to thank Lieutenant-Commander P. K. Kemp, R.N., Head of the Historical Section, and Commander N. P. E. Whitestone, R.N., of the Department of the Chief of Naval Information and now Naval Correspondent for the *Daily Telegraph,* for their help and kindness.

My thanks are also due to those authors who have written so excellently upon these stirring times. I should particularly like to mention Don Newton and A. Cecil Hampshire's *Taranto* (William Kimber); Kenneth Poolman's *Illustrious* (William Kimber); and Captain Pack's *The Battle of Matapan* (Batsford).

Finally, I must stress that any views or opinions expressed in this book are my own and do not represent those of anyone else.

JOHN WINGATE

# PREFACE

This book tells of the deeds of the Fleet Air Arm in the Mediterranean from the summer of 1940 to the spring of 1941 in the Second World War. During that short period, a handful of naval fliers revolutionised war at sea.

The story centres on the aircrew of a Swordfish Torpedo-Spotter Reconnaissance aircraft. Its crew, Sub-Lieutenant Bill Tanner and Midshipman (A) Brander, and their Divisional Officer, Lieutenant-Commander Kyne, are entirely fictitious characters.

For the rest I have endeavoured to give as authentic a setting as possible to this particularly glorious chapter in the story of the Fleet Air Arm. In doing so I have received much help from many of the distinguished officers who played a part in it. If, however, I have inadvertently done less than justice to any of those mentioned in my story, I offer them my sincere apologies.

I wish, in particular, to thank Commander Norman Kennedy, D.S.C., Royal Navy, who gave much technical assistance; Captain Kenneth Williamson, D.S.O., Royal Navy, the Squadron Commander who led the attack upon Taranto; for his invaluable help, Admiral Sir Robin Bridge, K.B.E., C.B., Captain of the grand old H.M.S. *Eagle* who 'carried the can' until she could serve no more; and, finally Admiral Sir Denis Boyd, K.C.B., C.B.E., D.S.C., who was so generous with his encouragement and friendship.

It is to the genius of Admiral Boyd and to his gallant fliers that this book is dedicated, in all humility.

Lastly I must record the words of the greatest sailor of them all, the man who turned Mussolini's *Mare Nostrum* into Cunningham's Pond: the late Admiral of the Fleet, Viscount Cunningham of Hyndhope, K.T., G.C.B., O.M., D.S.O. Encouraging me to write this book, he wrote shortly before he died:

*I don't doubt that the youth of the country know little of what the Navy did for the country during the late war; the tendency is to forget all about it as a nasty dream and with little about it worth remembering.*

*While you are writing these stories of naval operations, I would ask you to look into the evacuation of Greece and the operations round the evacuation of Crete. In my opinion (as I hope I showed in my despatch) the wonderful spirit of the sailors, both of the Navy and the Merchant Navy, is an example never surpassed of fortitude and tenacity when nearly dead beat.*

*Andrew Cunningham.*

# CHAPTER 1

*Seek and Destroy*

'Start the attack!'

Sub-Lieutenant William Tanner, pilot of E7Q, the only Swordfish from Malta in the squadron, saw the shaded blue light winking at him from ahead. He heard his observer yelling at him through the Gosport tube. At last they had reached the target area. The leading sub-flight was breaking formation. He could see the Squadron Commander, 'Lofty' Truman, in E4A, diving already.

'Hold your hat on!' Bill Tanner shouted down the speaking-tube. 'We're going in, Brandy…'

The Swordfish to starboard swung away, then began its dive. Bill gripped the stick and eased down the nose of his torpedo bomber. He had absolute confidence in the C.O., Lieutenant-Commander Henry Truman. Laconic, tall and gangling, Truman was an experienced professional. He knew his job; he loved the Swordfish Torpedo-Spotter Reconnaissance biplane. He was also a Navy cricketer, hockey and rugger player. The stubbly hair that sprouted from his stooping head, the monkey ears that stuck out sideways, and his expansive, generous features endeared him to the wild young men he led. Standing at six foot, four inches, he was known irreverently as 'Lofty'. No one had yet discovered how he fitted into his cockpit.

Truman was leading this attack. In three sub-flights, the nine Swordfish were creeping up on Augusta at dusk. They had taken off from *Eagle*'s flight deck at 1850, E7Q joining them from Malta, and had been in the air for two hours.

The smouldering cone of Etna loomed high above them now, glowing red in the gathering dusk.

They were running out of height when suddenly Bill saw ahead the black mass of Sicily, its mountains rising sheer from the sea. Taormina was just visible due north, a white necklace sprinkled atop its pinnacle of rock; Catania lay in the blue haze ahead, and now, sweeping up below them, came the port of Augusta, their target. Bill felt his head suddenly clear.

'Can you see 'em?' he yelled through the tube to Brandy.

Bill saw in his mind Brandy's owl-like face peering over the edge of the observer's cockpit. Midshipman (A) Brander was an irrepressible character, full of bounce and humour. With black eyes in a round face, and with his squat, powerful body, he shambled along like an ape. But groping one's way back to Hal Far airfield on Malta was what mattered, and Brandy was a competent observer. The air gunner had been substituted for long-range fuel tanks.

Bill searched the darkness but could see little until, quite suddenly, the breakwaters stretched towards them.

'One destroyer and one tanker, fine on your port bow,' Brandy shouted. 'Can't see the cruisers.'

They were down to a thousand feet now, about three miles off. It was a clear, fine evening and the town with its battlements stood up starkly.

Tanner was watching the shaded blue lights on Truman's tail. Then the lantern winked: Vic One and Two take the destroyer; Vic Three, the tanker. Executive signal.

It might have been a peacetime exercise, except that the destroyer was opening fire. Red and green tracer drifted slowly up to meet them.

Truman was well into his dive now, while Vic Three, under Jake Matson, had sheered away to starboard to attack the tanker.

Bill glanced at the altimeter: eighty feet. He had to lose another fifty before dropping his torpedo. He forced down his nose and saw the glassy surface of the sea rushing up to meet him.

Captain Robin Bridge — 'Daddy' to his officers — felt desperately tired as he leant over the bridge-rail of the old carrier. Since the 9th of July 1940, *Eagle* had been manoeuvring to operate her continuous anti-submarine patrols. Her antediluvian Swordfish had formed a permanent umbrella over the Mediterranean fleet which, once again, the Commander-in-Chief Admiral Sir Andrew Cunningham had taken to sea in search of the enemy.

The Captain smiled to himself as he watched 824 Squadron warming up on the unarmoured steel deck. This was the Torpedo Squadron: between the wheels of each aircraft he could see the gleaming steel-blue torpedoes. What a contrast this scene must be to what was going on in the Italian fleet!

For two days the Italian Admiral had twisted and turned to elude his adversary. Admiral Cunningham ('A.B.C.' as he was affectionately known throughout the fleet) had one purpose only: to destroy the enemy. Yet, with his slower battleships — *Warspite* (his flagship), *Malaya* and *Royal Sovereign* — he could never overtake his slippery and faster foe ... and this was where *Eagle* came in.

Her Swordfish torpedo bombers were to cripple or slow down the enemy battleships. Her few obsolescent Gladiators, under the leadership of the Commander (Flying) Keighly-Peach, were to drive off enemy air attacks. Thus, in theory, the

Commander-in-Chief would one day lay his battle fleet alongside that of the enemy — once the Fleet Air Arm, as yet unbloodied, had struck.

*Phoenix,* an Italian submarine on patrol, had first reported on July 8th that the British battle fleet had made its way into the Mediterranean. Since the Italians had so treacherously entered the war by joining Hitler, Admiral Cunningham had been spoiling for a fight. He first, however, had to arrange for the neutralisation of the French fleet, and now that the tragic happenings of Oran and Dakar were events of the past, the sole naval contestants in the Mediterranean were the Italians and the Royal Navy.

Weeks of continuous bombing, weeks of air operations, and now there had been two abortive days in which the enemy battle fleet had slipped through the net again, in spite of Debenham's heroic attack with his squadron on an 8-inch cruiser. But now, even as the nine Swordfish at 1145 had winged towards the enemy battle fleet, the shadowing flying boat 5807 had been forced to return to Malta because she was running out of fuel. The reconnaissance Swordfish had also lost the enemy; air touch had not been regained until 1215, when Flying Boat 5803 had reported the Italians.

The torpedo bombers had not found the battleship they were after; instead, at 1330, they had sighted a concentration of large ships steering north. Lofty Truman unhesitatingly led his three sub-flights into the attack. He was making history: this was the first torpedo bomber attack from carrier-based aircraft ever to be launched in wartime. They flew through intensive anti-aircraft fire and, having worked round to the westward, they attacked the rear ship of the starboard column.

'We might have hit one, sir,' Truman had reported laconically, after landing on at 1434, 'but they didn't hit us.'

The Squadron Commander had saluted and turned on his heel to return to the refuelling and re-arming of his torpedo bombers.

That had been twenty-four hours ago. The enemy had turned and run, and there was a feeling of frustration in the fleet. *Eagle*'s Captain had sensed this when he'd taken a rapid look round the ship on this morning, the 10th of July. His sailors felt cheated.

The fleet had withdrawn to avoid possible enemy submarine attack. After cruising south-east of Malta through the night and during the forenoon, to give time for the destroyers to refuel, the fleet had steamed north again. Twilight had stolen over the Mediterranean, and now it was *Eagle*'s turn; once more the 'air boys' could show their mettle.

The Captain turned towards the orange streak on the western horizon, where lingered the last light of sunset. The squadron should be approaching its targets about now. He could see in his imagination the sleepy port, the cruisers alongside the breakwaters. He closed his eyes. If the Swordfish failed to achieve surprise, the attack would be suicidal. Time dragged, but the hours passed.

The Captain sank down on to the bridge seat. The silhouettes of *Malaya* and *Royal Sovereign* slid rapidly past his port side as *Eagle* swung to her helm. He glanced over his starboard quarter. His faithful watchdogs, the destroyers *Vampire* and *Voyager,* were still there, perfectly in station. They had not been busy, except during the air-raids two days ago. Incredibly no Swordfish had been seriously damaged as yet.

The Captain glanced over his shoulder as his bulky Chief Yeoman of Signals loomed up beside him. '*Immediate*, sir.'

The Captain read the signal, then moved swiftly to the centre of the compass platform. 'Full ahead together,' he snapped.

'Emergency landing-on procedure. Two T.S.R. reported badly damaged.' He turned towards the lanky figure of the Commander (Flying), who had appeared behind him. 'Report when you're ready, Commander.'

'Aye, aye, sir. Permission to test the *Affirmative*?'

'Yes.'

The Captain turned towards the after funnel. The shaded blue lights glowed in the dusk. He glanced down at the flight deck where the landing-on lights glimmered. Those weeks of night-flying training were paying off now. He could see the fire-fighting teams crouching in the netting along the sides. The First Aid parties were out too; he could distinguish the P.M.O. and the young 'Doc' waiting with their stretcher parties on either side of the flight deck.

*Eagle* waited for her lame ducks. The Captain sighed as he glanced once again at the crumpled signal he'd fished from his pocket: the squadron must have had a bad time at Augusta. He'd know soon who had survived.

He turned round suddenly to listen. Was that the drone of approaching engines? And if so, why was the sound so low down on the horizon?

The Captain's heart leapt. Enemy aircraft, perhaps, and torpedo bombers at that?

'Alarm port!' he yelled. 'Stand by all guns!'

# CHAPTER 2

*Disaster*

Though Bill Tanner felt no fear, a strange numbness had come over him. He could not analyse his feelings. He only knew he had a job to do and must concentrate. If he did as he'd been trained during these weeks, he might survive.

The dark line of the breakwater swept under his nose, and then, as he watched the C.O. jinking ahead of him, he eased back the stick. There must have been an A.A. emplacement on the breakwater, for flak was streaming up at him from beneath the belly of the Swordfish. The destroyer, too, was now firing everything she had. Yellow, red and green tracer were curling incredibly slowly towards him, then crossing ahead and swinging away astern.

The target was barely a thousand yards away and straight ahead of him. He eased the throttle and watched the speed walking rapidly back... 107, 100, 95... lined up now like an exercise, except for the flak; and the enemy was not using searchlights, thank God...

90 knots... He stopped throwing the machine about. Steadied her... Suddenly the destroyer stood up like a house against the light as her guns flamed. Ahead, the C.O. swooped upwards, his burden released. Mesmerised, Bill watched the splash of the torpedo, saw the bubbling wake as the 'fish' raced true towards its target. There she was, right ahead... He pressed his torpedo-release grip, and the electromagnets released their load. The plane leapt as the torpedo jettisoned.

Bill could see nothing: he was too busy hauling the shag-bat to port, away from the flying metal. His last memory was of the destroyer, her guns blazing, jerking suddenly. There was an orange flash, a gush of black smoke, and then the flames licked. As he pulled away, he saw Truman ahead of him, dipping and weaving towards the breakwater. Why the devil hadn't he tried to gain height, away from all this flying metal?

'We've hit her, we've ruddy well hit her! She's broken in half!' Brandy was yelling over the Gosport tube. Bill saw a red flash beneath the C.O.'s belly. For a moment it looked as if E4A was about to become a blazing torch: flames had begun licking along the leader's fuselage, and smoke was trailing from his engine.

Bill dragged his Swordfish away, up and over the advancing breakwater. Then, as he looked down, he saw an astonishing sight. Truman's observer, Hugh Garnett, was standing up in the observer's cockpit, as if he were on a peacetime exercise. He was slapping at the flames with his gloved hands, beating out the fire. The licking flames quivered, went out. Then came the tragedy. Hugh gave a jerk, stood stiffly for a brief instant, then flopped, half-hanging over the side of the fuselage. His arm was dangling in the slipstream.

'God! Hugh's hit!'

He heard Brandy swearing behind him, yelling that the tanker had also been torpedoed by Vic Three. Bill banked steeply and clawed for the night sky. The breakwater swung beneath him now as he looked back over his shoulder and down upon the scene.

Dante's Inferno would have been mild in comparison. The tanker was a white nucleus in a sea of flames. The wretched crew were leaping from her, choosing a burning sea in preference to her roasting plates. Oil blazed on the surface of the sea, its flames streaking across the black waters of the harbour.

The destroyer was settling already. Her bows were cocked into the air, while her stern had already settled as far as her waist. Courageously the after gun still kept firing, but its aim was ineffective.

It was at this moment that Bill's own worries struck him. He called up Brandy on the Gosport.

'Course for Malta?'

The flak beneath was intense, yet the tracer seemed noiseless, slow and unreal. It curled towards him and, as he watched, one red hosepipe seemed to hang longer than the rest. He was still mesmerised when Brandy shouted:

'Course 158 degrees until Syracuse is abeam, then alter —'

The observer never finished his sentence. There was a blue flash, a sizzling noise all about them, like the discharge of an electrical condenser. The stick jumped in Bill's hands, and he felt her nose go down. A rent appeared in the port wing, and then came the flailing of tattered canvas.

He wrenched at the stick and gingerly opened the throttle. Holding his breath, he braced himself for the dive into the sea as she stalled. Then suddenly, like a seagull gliding in the slipstream above the clifftops, she lifted her nose and gained flying speed.

'You O.K., Brandy?'

Nothing but the roar of the engine could be heard through the Gosport. Bill shouted again, but there was no reply.

He steadied her on 158 degrees as the flak died away. Taking his feet off the rudder bar he eased himself round to glance into the observer's cockpit, where he could see the top of Brandy's head. The long-range fuel tank was built in like a horseshoe, suicidally located just above the observer's skull.

Bill's heart missed a beat. The cockpit had been hit. There was a gash in the tank through which petrol was streaming. Brandy was hit — he must have been killed, or be unconscious.

'Brandy… Brandy, for God's sake, are you O.K.?'

The roar through the Gosport — nothing more. Bill turned back to his cockpit, then, bringing her on to course again, looked about him for the C.O. and for Syracuse. Ah! There was the promontory behind which the ancient Greek port sheltered. Towering above it, high in the sky, smouldered Etna. Syracuse lay five miles to starboard. Where was the C.O.?

For an instant panic swept over the young pilot. Suddenly he felt terribly alone. With nothing but the black night shielding him, the enemy — an angry, awakened hornets' nest — was searching the sky for him. His petrol reserves were draining away. Brandy lay dead or unconscious behind him… With a chilling shock Bill realised he hadn't memorised the course for Malta. Brandy had given him 158 degrees to Syracuse, but what was the course from Syracuse to Malta? He wished now that he'd taken more interest at the briefing, but he'd left it all to Brandy. *My job is just to fly the crate,* he had thought, *not to navigate.* What a stupid, incompetent so-and-so he'd been… and now he was to pay for his slackness with his life. He'd better search for the C.O.

He brought her round to port, his ear hyper-sensitive to the engine note; but she was running smoothly again, sweet as a nut. A thousand feet beneath him he saw the black expanse of water. Then he spotted a dim blue light and his heart leapt. Pushing the stick away from him, he began to lose height.

It was the shaded stern light of a 'Stringbag', as the Swordfish were nicknamed. After all these weeks of night training, he'd recognise that elusive blur anywhere. His eyes had ached frequently enough trying to follow it. He opened the throttle as he levelled off at three hundred feet. Slowly gaining on the Swordfish, he recognised the C.O.'s markings. Hugh's arm was still flapping over the side. He must be dead.

Bill flew up alongside and waved. The helmeted head turned quickly towards him. Truman waved back, then fumbled in the cockpit. A blue light winked slowly: *Return to Malta. Course two-one-o.*

Bill waved in acknowledgement. He saw Truman take his eyes from his instrument panel for a moment and shake his head at the sight of E7Q. Bill took station again on his C.O.'s port quarter, stacking up fifty feet to cover him. The light winked again: *Return to base and leave me. I will follow.*

Bill grinned in the loneliness of his cockpit. The dials glowed with their luminous paint, the air-speed indicator showing only eighty knots. No wonder he had been forced to throttle back: he was over-running the C.O. Truman must be nursing a damaged engine; probably half his cylinders were shot away.

*Good Lord! Look at my fuel gauge — it's barely half full!*

Bill had to think quickly. The C.O. was obviously in trouble. His observer was dead, his engine damaged and giving him barely eighty knots. Cloud was obscuring the stars now, and it was difficult to pick out the land from the horizon, let alone the sea. If the C.O. was left on his own, would he be able to find Malta any better than E7Q?

Bill flicked on his own lamp: *Is your compass O.K.? You are off course.*

The C.O.'s Morse blinked in reply: *Obey orders and return to base. I will follow.*

Bill eased back again on the throttle. The C.O. was almost on stalling speed. He could see Truman pointing south-westward.

Bill had to think quickly. If he stayed to cover the C.O. and lead him back to base, he himself might have to ditch.

He glanced again at the fuel gauge. The needle had dropped alarmingly. At this rate he'd barely make Malta. The petrol must be pouring from the reserve, thereby draining the wing tank. If he remained to cover Truman, he'd have to reduce speed, and this would mean he'd be longer in the air and would run dry.

*Do you read my order?* Truman's lamp blinked again. *Return to—*

Bill ignored the remainder of the signal. From the corner of his eye he was watching the C.O.'s gauntleted fist jerking to starboard, pointing south-west. Bill grinned. It was better thus, in company. They'd drown together. How the hell did the C.O. think Bill could leave him?

He opened the throttle and slowly drew ahead. When he was two hundred yards beyond, he drifted in slightly above Truman. He eased back the throttle and reduced gradually to the C.O.'s speed.

Syracuse was abeam now. Bill waggled his wings, turning slowly to starboard to 210 degrees. He grinned as he watched the C.O. drag his damaged Stringbag round. He was following.

Bill sighed, alone now with his thoughts, while three feet behind him lay Brandy. Ah! There was Cape Passaro, out ahead to starboard. Malta should be due south of the Cape, some seventy miles away, about forty-five minutes' flying. Bill glanced at the gauge — it had walked back further, even in these few minutes. He felt the clamminess of sweat inside his goggles. It was strange how, once you had to wait for death, you became frightened — in the heat of action you were numb, too busy to be scared. But now…

Where the devil were the others? They could give him a correct course: the observers couldn't *all* be dead. It was odd how they'd missed Dave Brinton, the third member of their vic. Perhaps he'd bought it in the flak. And what of Number Two Vic? Where'd they gone? They couldn't *all* have been lost, surely?

Bill found to his disgust that he was shivering, now that the excitement was over. In spite of the sweat, he felt ice cold with fear. This was his first action, and until now he'd always believed that death never claimed you; it was always the other chap who bought it.

He looked at his watch and could hardly believe his eyes. Only seven forty-five. Well, in an hour's time it would be all over...

'The attack on Augusta was successful. Two of our aircraft failed to return.' That was what the B.B.C. would say. A simple epitaph. Well, he'd done his best, in spite of what that swine Kyne thought. Lieutenant-Commander Kyne was the officer in charge of the Fleet Air Arm Sub-Lieutenants in Malta. A 'passed-over' officer, recalled for the duration, he was a much older man: in his forties, which was old for a naval officer. He'd earned his wings in the R.F.C. and he still yearned to fly. Perhaps this was what caused his jealousy of the youngsters, Bill thought. Kyne's sandy hair was greying at the temple and on his eyebrows, and this gave him a sharp, fox-like look.

He, Bill Tanner, Sub-Lieutenant, R.N., had never wanted to join the Fleet Air Arm. His father, a smashed-up R.F.C. pilot from the First War, had beseeched him not to volunteer for the air. Bill felt sad as he remembered seeing his mother's face after he'd broken the news that he'd been press-ganged. 'You promised me you wouldn't, Bill,' she had reproached him gently. She couldn't be expected to understand the mysterious ways of the Admiralty. War made ruthless demands: if too many pilots were being killed, more must be trained. Simple.

Only Kyne couldn't understand. Only Kyne refused to comprehend Bill's reluctance to volunteer. Yes, the man hated his guts. He always had, since cadet days at Dartmouth, when Bill had seen through him. Kyne had never acknowledged the injustice he had done Bill, but had known instinctively that he'd been wrong. He had thrashed Cadet Tanner, and the thrashing had been unjust. Bill had protested his innocence, but Term Officer Kyne had persisted in the punishment. 'Gutless and a liar,' had been his verdict. Unfortunate that they were rubbing shoulders again in Malta. Well, it would soon be over now, and Kyne could say he'd been right. Tanner was missing — inexperience and incompetence, obviously, just as Kyne had always suggested. Tanner's heart wasn't in it, that was what he'd say. How could he hope to survive? Pressed men were worse than useless: they upset morale.

Bill glanced at the gauge: nearly empty. He'd hear the Pegasus missing at any moment now. Better prepare to ditch. The air rushed past his ears as he looked over the side. Sicily was vanishing on his starboard quarter, and blackness lay ahead. He searched to port.

What was that? He blinked, peered again. Yes, a distinct 'A' in blue lights just below him. He strained his eyes and then quite suddenly, he saw the three wakes. Three streaks of bubbling foam, the central one bigger and thicker than the others.

He fumbled for his Verey's pistol as the first shell exploded just below him. There was a white flash, the aircraft trembled, and then a myriad of bullets came winging slowly towards him in criss-cross white and green tracer.

In the darkness his fingers were all thumbs. Trying to fly the crate and load a cartridge into the pistol was no easy matter. He fired the Verey's light over the port side. The green flare exploded, then floated down as the barrage once again opened up. The explosions had one use: they lit up the cockpit while he was fumbling for the Aldis.

Bill had been temporarily blinded by the brilliant flashes. He'd lost the illuminated *Affirmative* (the signal to land on) and the C.O. had disappeared. He banked steeply and began looking for Truman. There he was, five hundred feet below.

Bill trained his lamp. *E7Q calling C.O.*, he flashed. *After you.*

An 'R' winked back.

Suddenly it was very quiet. The barrage had ceased. Then he saw *Eagle*'s landing lights, a blue necklace strung along the flight deck, half a mile to port. *Better stay up here until the C.O. has landed. This will be trickier than landing at Hal Far.*

It was a vain thought. At that instant the engine coughed, spluttered, coughed again... then suddenly cut. His heart missed a beat as the unnatural silence enfolded him. *Things'll move swiftly now. Oh God, so near and yet so far... to be drowned now, in sight of home...*

He heard the whine in the struts as he glided down towards the landing lights; the whine increased in pitch until the scream jangled his nerves... He wrestled with her as he tightened his Sutton harness. *Mustn't let her stall or I'll spin right in. Wrench her nose up at the last second...*

Then he saw the carrier's outline, a darker mass against the black ocean. 150 feet now — he was level with her bridge; now he was below her flight deck; then suddenly the white wake was threshing just below him... rushing upwards, leaping for him...

He braced his legs for the shock, yanked at the stick to bring up her nose. He felt the carrier's rear on her tail, then glimpsed a destroyer close to starboard. There was a sudden jolt, a tearing, terrifying roar, and then the water swamped him. He felt a sudden pain between the eyes. *This is it,* he thought, but still kicked out with despairing strength. The jagged edge of a broken spar caught in his life jacket as he went under, dragged down by the plane. He tore at his harness. Terror gripped him. *Oh God! No, no…*

His lungs were bursting as he reached the surface. He lay there spent, gasping like a stranded fish. Slowly he got his bearings again, lying on his back to regain his strength. Then he remembered the distress flares. *Brandy…*

He fumbled in his sodden jacket, found the flare, jerked it away from himself and hurled it downwind. The calcium ignited in the water, spluttering smokily and erupting its light into the night. He groped on the other side of his life jacket. He'd keep the last flare until they were near him.

He turned towards where the tail had been. Brandy? Where was Brandy? Oh God, he'd gone down with the plane.

'There 'ee be! Hold on, mate, we've got 'ee!'

Bill heard the seaman's West Country hail. With tears welling uncontrollably into his eyes, he tried to raise his arm in acknowledgement. As he tore the last flare from his belt, he felt the rap of a heaving line across his face. The outline of a whaler bucketed above him. Burly arms reached down and helped him scramble into the boat, where he flopped down on to the bottom boards. Wiping the wetness from his face, he felt the stickiness of blood…

'Poor basket…'

Distantly Bill heard the greeting. Nausea overwhelmed him as his thoughts whirled. Then blackness engulfed him and he knew no more.

# CHAPTER 3

*Naval Discipline*

It was difficult for a young, wounded Fleet Air Arm pilot, lying in one of *Eagle*'s sick bay cots, to realise that Operation M.A.5 (or the Action off Calabria, as they now called it) had been brought to a successful conclusion.

The safe and timely arrivals of the fast convoy M.F.1 and slow convoy M.S.1 from Malta was the prime object of the operation, and this had now been achieved. The Commander-in-Chief had hoped to lure out the enemy while the Mediterranean fleet covered the convoys. The opposing fleets had engaged briefly, but the fight had terminated when the Italians ran for home. The Malta convoys had got through safely, in spite of the heavy and accurate bombing of the last two days.

'What day is it, Doc?'

Bill saw the doctor's gentle face peering down at him.

'The 15th of July. We're just in.'

Bill watched the patterns of reflected sunlight dappling the deckhead in the pastel-green sick bay. He felt the luxury of clean sheets.

'Where are we?'

'Back in Alex. You're a fraud.' The Doc was laughing. 'You've missed the worst.'

'How d'you mean?'

'The Eyeties have been bombing hell out of us all the way home. They've been plastering this poor old ship for the past two days, since the night we picked you out of the drink. Listen to this despatch from C.-in-C.'

Bill heard the rustle of signal paper, then Luke read aloud:

*'I cannot conclude my remarks without a reference to H.M.S. Eagle. This obsolescent aircraft carrier, with only 17 Swordfish embarked, found and kept touch with the enemy fleet, and flew off two striking forces of nine torpedo bombers within the space of four hours, both of which attacked, and all aircraft returned. Twenty-four hours later a torpedo striking force was launched on shipping in Port Augusta and throughout the five days' operation Eagle maintained constant A/S patrols in daylight and carried out several searches. Much of Eagle's aircraft operating work was done in the fleeting intervals between, and even during bombing attacks and I consider her performance reflects great credit on her Commanding Officer.'*

'What d'you think of that, Tanner?'

The words had sunk in only slowly. He wanted to ask so many questions, to know so much.

'Better get some sleep. You've had quite a smack across the head.'

Bill felt the bandages, but his eyes still held a question.

'You're all right,' the Doc said. 'You're indestructible, with that thick skull.'

'Brandy?'

'He's fine too. Just a clock on the forehead. He passed out from loss of blood.'

'Thank God.' Bill fell silent, his brain whirling. It was difficult to arrest the floating sensation, to fix one's thoughts.

'The C.O.?'

'I'm fine.'

Bill slowly turned his head on the pillow. A tall Lieutenant-Commander stood by his cot, his cap tucked under his arm.

Humorous eyes twinkled from beneath a craggy brow, and large ears stuck out from a huge head.

'Thanks for your help, Bill. You O.K.?' The 'two-and-a-half' glanced at the surgeon, who nodded. 'See you later, then. Just wanted to thank you.' The large face smiled, then began to lose focus.

'Is Hugh Garnett O.K., sir?' Bill whispered. 'Your observer?' Things were going hazy now. From far away he heard the C.O.'s voice:

'Hugh's dead.'

Bill turned his head away, needing the comfort and privacy of his pillow. He focussed his eyes on a scuttle opposite, on the ship's side. Slowly the truth registered. Then mercifully semi-consciousness claimed him again, sparing him further pain.

It was exactly eight weeks before Bill Tanner was fit again for flying duties. Four weeks in hospital; two weeks leave in the rest camp, where he was thoroughly miserable; and, finally, two weeks' light duty which left him dispirited. It was grand, therefore, to be in the air again.

This was his third day's flying. The 'boys' had welcomed him back, but with a strange reserve. Something was being withheld from him. Things weren't right.

'Where are we, Brandy?' he called through the Gosport tube. 'Time to go home yet?' It was good to feel the wind again, good to feel his new Swordfish responding even better than his old crate.

'Alter course to 1350 in three minutes, Bill,' the cheery voice boomed. 'It's good to be sitting behind a lunatic again.'

'Repeat?'

'It's good to be chauffeured by a lunatic again.'

'Thanks. Thought that's what you said.' Bill shoved the stick forward and plunged to sea level. He heard the whine of the struts, revelled in the sudden freedom. God! It was wonderful to be up again… He pulled the stick back and sent her floundering upwards, until she stood on her tail. It was a matter of honour for Brandy to maintain silence, but Bill heard him swearing. The observer had lost his dividers in the sudden dive.

'Alter course to 135 degrees,' the Midshipman shouted. 'That is, if you can read.'

Bill looked back over his shoulder, saw Lofty Truman away to the northward. Like old times. It was grand to be back.

Twenty minutes later they landed as a sub-flight on the desert airstrip which the squadron was using while *Eagle* was in Alexandria. Bill would miss them all when he was sent back to Malta. It was a quarter past twelve when Bill finally preceded Brandy up the officers' gangway of the old carrier towering above him. Yes, it was good to be asked on board. He put his hands on the wires of the gangway and hauled himself upwards.

At the head of the gangway stood the gangway staff. In an opening on the port side, at the forward end of the quarterdeck, was the Quartermaster's lobby. Here the ship's daily harbour routine was organised. Bill heard again the whine of the fans as he looked at *Eagle*'s crest painted proudly on the enamelled lifebuoy, which was on a wooden stand facing him, while behind it, on mahogany scrolls, were emblazoned her battle honours. Would Calabria count, he wondered? Would Augusta? Or didn't aircraft strikes qualify yet as battles?

He saw the Bo'sun's Mate saluting, and next to him the Royal Marine Corporal. The Quartermaster, his chain looped round his neck, held his Bo'sun's call in his left hand and came to attention as Bill stepped down from the gangway. Behind him stood the Officer of the Watch, telescope tucked beneath his left arm; it was Ralph Henderson, and he was grinning as he saluted.

'Good to see you,' the young Sub said. 'Good to be up again?'

'You bet. It's been a long time. Wish I was coming with you.'

It was sticky here in Alex, in spite of their tropical rig. Bill was turning to leave the lobby when he heard a syrupy voice behind him. He'd have recognised that sneer anywhere.

'Ah! Sub-Lieutenant Tanner,' said Kyne. 'May I have a word with you?'

Bill turned on his heel and saluted. What was Kyne doing on *Eagle*? Taking passage, probably.

'Sir?'

Lieutenant-Commander Anthony Kyne, Royal Navy, was smiling with his mouth but not with his pale eyes. In his immaculate white shirt, shorts and stockings; with his starched cap-cover and whitened buckskin shoes; with his faded shoulder epaulettes denoting his seniority as a two-and-a-half, Kyne glanced disapprovingly at the grease-smeared pilot.

'The Base Commander wants to see you ashore — and you'd better square yourself off. You're hardly a credit to the Branch.'

'Yes, sir.' Bill felt his anger stirring as he passed an oily hand across his hair. 'What time, sir?'

'After lunch: two-thirty.'

Bill hesitated. There was still time to visit the ward room. Then he blurted out: 'What's it about, sir?'

He saw the gleam of triumph in Kyne's eyes as he paused, a bundle of signals clutched in his left hand. 'Investigation of your crash. You're on the mat, and I've been checking up on the report of proceedings. You're being charged, Tanner.'

'What for, sir?'

Bill clenched his fists and stared Kyne squarely in the eye, but the senior officer was already turning to leave the ship.

'Disobedience, Tanner,' he muttered as he pushed past Bill. 'Direct disobedience of orders.'

The afternoon sunlight, striking obliquely upon the placid surface of Alexandria harbour, was reflected upwards upon the white, cork-painted deckhead of the Captain's day cabin. A long-bladed fan rotated lazily from the deckhead, and beneath it sat two middle-aged men in armchairs. The Commander (E) wore the purple of the Engineer between his stripes, while opposite him, smoking his pipe and watching the blue clouds dissipating near the fan, lounged the Captain.

'Are you absolutely sure, Chief?' *Eagle*'s Captain asked. His was a stern face, but when he smiled the crow's feet at the corners of his eyes softened its granite.

''Fraid so, sir. That's why I've come to you. I've drafted a signal.' He handed the slip of pink paper across to the older man. He read it irritably.

*Secret. Immediate. C.-in-C., M.E.D. Alexandria, repeated C.-in-C. Med. from Eagle. Petrol lines seriously damaged by bombing of 11th July, but defect has only recently become apparent. Suspect rust and dirt in the system which prevents safe operation of aircraft. Request immediate survey. T.O.O. 1405/1st October.*

Captain Bridge felt cheated. After all the old girl had come through: the attacks in North Africa, Greece, Augusta, the bombings, and now this — out of action, probably because of near misses. She'd never been hit directly, but the poor old thing was so old that even her tanks were rusting through.

'Well, Chief, there it is.' He looked up and smiled sadly. 'But I hate to think what Andrew will say.'

'He'll be summoning you, sir, before the day's much older,' the Chief laughed. 'What'll the fleet do without the old girl?'

The Captain nodded. The fleet needed the Air Arm these days.

'Thank God Denis Boyd's arrived safely,' he said. 'Only just in time.'

'Where's *Illustrious* now, sir?'

'Malta. Good show, that Benghazi strike of hers.'

'The seventeenth of September, wasn't it?' the Chief asked. The Captain nodded, before the Commander (E) continued, 'Yes, fine effort. Looking to her laurels after our Tobruk attack, sir.' They both laughed, and then the Captain glanced at his watch.

'If this petrol defect can't be remedied by Alex dockyard, Chief, does it mean returning to the U.K.?'

Commander (E) nodded. 'Malta can't do it, sir, under today's conditions. With the bombing there, it would take months to complete; it's a big job. All the piping has to be stripped out of the ship.'

'In fact, Chief,' the Captain continued, lowering his voice, 'the attack on Taranto is becoming remote for us, isn't it?'

The Chief nodded. 'Sorry, sir,' he said. 'You know, if there was anything I could do…'

The Captain smiled. 'That's all right. Better make sure as many Stringbags are airworthy as possible. We'll lend *Illustrious* our boys. They'll show them how to fly…' The Captain glanced at his watch and hauled himself from his chair. 'Now

I'd better go and tell C. in C.' he said looking at his grey-haired Chief. 'Andrew won't like it at all, Chief. He won't like it at all.'

Lieutenant-Commander Truman had arrived at the Commander of the Base's office just on time. He'd been summoned from Eagle's hangar to this investigation in his capacity as C.O. of the squadron, but he hated every moment of it. He wouldn't have brought the charge. But, in a way, that chap Kyne was right in insisting: after all, Tanner had flouted naval discipline. You couldn't have everyone thinking he was a Nelson.

Truman stood up with the others as the Commander of the Base entered the crowded office. He was heavily built, dark and putting on weight.

Diagonally across one corner was a desk. Behind it were ranged three chairs. The middle one was empty, and behind the others stood two officers. The Secretary pulled back the central chair.

The Commander crossed the anteroom and stood for a moment, his hands on the back of his chair.

'I've called you together,' he said, 'to investigate a serious charge brought against Sub-Lieutenant Tanner by Lieutenant-Commander Kyne.'

Truman watched intently as the Base Commander picked his words.

'I have convened this investigation to help me decide whether there are sufficient grounds for me to institute official proceedings for a Board of Enquiry.' He turned to his right, to the mild man in black spectacles. 'I will ask the Secretary to read the charge.'

The slight figure nodded. The sheet of foolscap he was holding rustled in front of them.

'Sub-Lieutenant William Tanner of Hal Far, Malta, is hereby charged with directly disobeying the order of the Commanding Officer of Squadron 813 in that he, Sub-Lieutenant Tanner did on the 10th of July' — the Secretary paused for breath and squinted over his glasses at the young officer standing before him — 'deliberately ignore the order of his Commanding Officer to return immediately to Malta.'

Lieutenant-Commander Truman caught his breath in the silence that followed. He was watching, like everyone else, the white-faced Fleet Air Arm pilot standing so rigidly to attention. *Thank heavens he's shifted into clean tropical rig,* thought Truman; the base wallahs were sticklers for correct dress. Quite right too: smart men meant a smart ship, and a smart ship brought efficiency, which in turn bred high morale. They needed their self-respect in these exhausting days; their lives depended upon their fighting efficiency.

'Sit down.'

*He's trying to reduce the tension,* Truman thought. *He's taken off his cap; I'd better do the same. There's Tanner following suit. I can hear his sigh of relief: it's not so official now — more like a family gathering to see who's pinched the apples…*

'Would you like to tell us what happened, Tanner?' the Commander asked quietly.

Tanner, still pale from his sojourn in hospital, rose smartly to his feet. He held himself well; his sandy hair was cut short on a head set proudly atop firmly braced shoulders. *No flies on him,* thought Truman. *Good luck, Tanner. Don't lose your temper, boy. That's your danger: if Kyne needles you too much, you'll explode. The Commander wouldn't like that.*

Bill Tanner started to tell his story. He spoke quietly but clearly; obviously he was telling the truth. Truman smiled to himself. This young pilot was as laconic as his C.O.: the recounting of the Augusta raid sounded as if the attack was a peacetime night exercise.

'And so I waited for the C.O. to land on, sir, but I ditched just short of the ship.'

'Why?' the Commander of the Base asked.

'My tank was dry, sir.'

'How d'you know?'

'The reserve tank was hit in the attack, sir. I could see petrol streaming from it when we were struck.'

The Commander nodded. 'Midshipman Brander was your observer?'

'Yes, sir.'

'Midshipman Brander…' The Commander was now addressing the squat Midshipman (A), who had jumped to his feet. His shorts and shirt were too small for him, and he looked hot and embarrassed.

'Sir?'

'You were Sub-Lieutenant Tanner's observer?'

'Yes, sir.'

'What happened after the attack on Augusta?'

'I don't really know, sir.'

The Commander paused at the murmur amongst the officers. His craggy eyebrows arched imperceptibly.

'I was knocked out, sir. I knew nothing after the fish — sorry, sir — after the torpedo dropped. The next thing I remember was the water lapping around me as the aircraft went down under us.'

'That's all?'

'That's all, sir.'

'Thank you.' The Commander was scribbling on a sheet of paper. Then Truman heard his name called.

'Sir?' He rose to his feet. His pulse quickened: he detested making a spectacle of himself. He saw the Commander's blue eyes peering up at him.

'What happened?'

'I ordered my sub-flight to attack the destroyer, sir, the others to deal with the tanker…'

'Yes?'

'We torpedoed the destroyer…'

'Any opposition?'

'There was some flak, sir.'

The Commander nodded. 'Go on.'

'I was hit when clearing the breakwater.' Truman snatched at the words; he could see the Commander was losing patience. 'My observer was killed, sir, so I had no course to steer.'

'Why didn't you follow the others?'

'I realised I would slow them down, sir. My engine had been hit and was coughing. Anyway, we'd been dispersed during the attack, sir, and we'd lost touch.'

He went on to describe the sequence of events: Tanner's assistance, his coverage, his… yes, unselfishness. He'd never known that Tanner was running on low fuel. Then came the crucial question:

'Did he, or did he not, disobey your order to leave you and return to Malta?'

Truman hesitated. There could be no evasion of the issue.

'I don't know whether he received the order, sir. I got no acknowledgement.'

'Thank you, Lieutenant-Commander Truman. Sit down, please.' The Commander turned again to the young pilot: 'Sub-Lieutenant Tanner… did you deliberately break visual contact with your C.O.?'

In the silence that followed, Truman watched Kyne. In the tension, the passed-over 'two-and-a-half' sprawled in his chair, his legs crossed. There was a half-smile on his lips, but his fingers tapped restlessly on the arm of the chair. Truman heard the sigh that escaped Kyne as Tanner spoke:

'Yes, sir.' The reply was defiant.

*Careful, Bill…* This youngster was challenging tradition. The older man was steeped in the inflexibility of naval discipline, accepted without question since his *Britannia* days when the old training ship had still lain at her buoys in the Dart.

The Commander looked at Tanner impersonally. 'Would you repeat your performance if you were faced again with the same predicament? Now that you realise the gravity of this charge?'

*For God's sake, Bill… watch it… now's your chance. Use your intelligence, boy,* Lofty Truman prayed. *Can't you see you can withdraw now with honour? Look at that two-faced Kyne — he's licking his chops…*

'Yes, I would, sir. Of course I would.'

Truman heard the brass clock ticking on the bulkhead. He saw the older man turn his face away.

'Anything to add?' the Commander asked perfunctorily. He was finished with the youth.

Tanner shook his head. 'No, thank you, sir.' He was whispering now. Then suddenly, as he was sitting down, Tanner said, 'The C.O. would have done the same for me, sir.'

The Commander's head jerked up, his eyes glinting angrily. Then he turned towards Kyne.

'You brought the charge, Lieutenant-Commander Kyne?'

The elegant figure in pressed shirt and shorts climbed slowly to his feet.

'Yes, sir, I did.'

'Why?'

The question was a pistol shot from the Commander's lips. Truman felt the skin prickling at the back of his neck.

'I'm responsible for the Sub-Lieutenants' discipline in Malta, sir. Orders can't be directly disobeyed, sir.'

'No.'

'And if a Sub-Lieutenant is deliberately disobeying his senior officer, then I must take action.'

'Certainly.'

Truman pressed his lips together.

'How did you know that Sub-Lieutenant Tanner had broken V/S contact?' the Commander asked Kyne.

'I was reading the pilot's reports, sir, and I asked Tanner to clarify his actions.' Kyne was speaking rapidly now, his words smooth and effortless.

'You took this up with his C.O.?'

'Yes, sir. I considered this action tantamount to mutiny.'

The unpleasant word shocked the assembly into silence. Then, looking directly at Kyne, the Commander said quietly:

'Lieutenant-Commander Kyne, you have no right to state your opinion. How I may eventually consider Sub-Lieutenant Tanner's action is for me only to decide.' The carefully chosen words cut through the proceedings like a knife. 'You may be seated.' The Commander's tone changed abruptly as he turned towards the Squadron Commander. 'Before I come to a decision, Lieutenant-Commander Truman, would you, as Tanner's Commanding Officer, like to add anything in mitigation?'

Truman climbed deliberately to his feet.

'Thank you, sir. I would.' He glanced momentarily at Kyne, then turned resolutely to face the Captain. 'Tanner saved my life, sir,' he said. 'Without him I should have lost my way and eventually been forced to ditch, with no hope of rescue. He covered me, and gave me my course, knowing full well he was running out of petrol. Finally, sir, he waited for me to land on.'

Truman felt himself colouring in his anger. He was again facing Kyne now, but he knew his words were still rational: 'This officer, sir is accusing one of my pilots of a grave charge. True, Tanner deliberately disobeyed me. But for a pretty good motive, sir, I submit.'

He sat down slowly. He felt better now. They could make what they liked of it. He watched the Commander hauling himself to his feet.

'Wait here a minute, please, gentlemen.' He turned towards the Paymaster Commander and the Secretary. 'Come with me, please,' he said quietly, as he led the way through to his inner office. He glanced back at the young pilot, who was now standing up respectfully. He spoke over his shoulder to the gathering of officers.

'We'll be back in a moment with our findings. Sit down, please, gentlemen.'

# CHAPTER 4

*'Illustrious', her name...*

In the vast harbour of Alexandria, the aircraft carrier lay swinging to her buoy. *Illustrious*, the first of the armoured-deck carriers, had joined the Mediterranean fleet.

Guarding the western gate of the Mediterranean was Vice-Admiral Sir James Somerville with his Force H. He flew his flag in the great battle cruiser *Hood*, and had in his command the aircraft carrier *Ark Royal*, the battleships *Valiant* and *Resolution* ('old Rezzo'); the old cruisers *Enterprise* and *Delhi;* the cruisers *Arethusa* and *Sheffield;* the destroyers *Duncan, Isis, Foxhound, Forester* and *Firedrake;* and the senior officer, Captain 'D' of the 8th Flotilla, with 18 destroyers. This was already a famous and redoubtable force.

At the other end of the Mediterranean prowled Admiral Cunningham with his Med fleet. At the end of August, *Illustrious* had come to join him.

On September 16th, her Commanding Officer, Captain Denis Boyd, was taking his evening constitutional at the after end of the flight deck: a good time, for there were not many people about. He stood alone by the round-down. A small man, compact and tough, he had the bearing of a natural athlete. As he stood on the flight deck, the White Ensign flapping lazily above him in the light airs, he felt his depression lifting. Things could be much worse.

He glanced across the harbour and smiled to himself. In less than a fortnight, the enemy had already had ample cause to regret *Illustrious*'s arrival. She had bombed Cagliari on passage to Malta, and this evening she was off once more — to bomb Benghazi, to attack the ships in harbour, and generally to annoy the Italians.

He took off his cap and tucked it beneath his arm. His short, stubbly hair accentuated the aggressive tilt of his head upon his square shoulders. A row of medal ribbons lent a splash of colour to the sombre uniform. He extracted his pouch and began to fill his pipe: time for a smoke before sunset, and before Williamson and Hale came to see him.

It seemed months since he'd first joined the ship at Barrow, launched her, whipped her into shape on passage to Bermuda and back; months since leaving Scapa Flow with *Valiant* in that panic rush. He smiled ruefully: he'd not even said goodbye to his wife, let alone celebrated their silver wedding. Rear Admiral Lumley Lyster, R.A., Aircraft Carriers, Mediterranean, had hoisted his flag in *Illustrious* just before sailing. A wonderful man, champion of the Fleet Air Arm, yet it was difficult sometimes to have an Admiral breathing down one's neck.

Captain Boyd watched a motor boat chugging across the turquoise water. The evening cloud was beginning to bank up from the west. It would be a good flying night. Boyd took a deep breath. He felt lucky to be alive.

The Captain was no sentimentalist, but he possessed an inner calm. Believing in his Maker, he could face all terrors and hardships. Perhaps, he thought, he had been shielded in his many dangers for this very job, vital and exhausting as it was likely to prove.

Denis Boyd had first requested permission to fly in 1911, shortly after Captain Murray Sueter had formed the Air Department of the Navy. Lieutenant-Commander Samson had allowed Boyd to fly his first Bristol pusher aircraft at Eastchurch in 1911.

The Captain smiled; yes, it was a long time ago. They only took three pilots a year in those days, and as he was number 19 on the list of volunteers, he had not been accepted by 1914 when the Great War broke out. He'd joined destroyers and been appointed in command of an 'oily wad' T.B.D., from which he was press-ganged to do a long course in torpedoes. He qualified as a 'Torps', then volunteered for submarines and spent the rest of the war in the 'K' boats, those 'down-funnel' suicide boats…

Later, in 1930, had come his chance to work for the future of a Fleet Air Arm, till then crippled by inter-service jealousies, political apathy and prejudice from within the Royal Navy itself.

Boyd frowned in his loneliness: a Captain's life was isolated, remote. He turned and glanced down the long flight deck with its lifts fore and aft. She was a fine ship, and there was no doubt what A.B.C. intended her role to be: the eyes of the fleet and its striking force. She must locate and cripple the enemy battle fleet so that ponderous and older British battleships could catch up and engage, broadside for broadside; she must harass and destroy the enemy fleet in harbour; she must bomb her supply ports.

Boyd's jaw set. Benghazi: that was where he'd be sending his gallant airmen tomorrow night. He pursed his lips as he gazed upon the lone Swordfish parked by number one lift. The Stringbag, that archaic but wonderful flying maid-of-all-work: reconnaissance, torpedo bomber, bomber and anti-submarine. It was no wonder her fliers loved her.

Ah! Here were two of the best strolling towards him now: Lieutenant-Commanders Williamson and Hale.

'Good evening, Ken; hullo, Ginger.'

'Good evening, sir.'

The C.O.s of Squadrons 815 and 819 shared a common characteristic: reticence and quietness, almost to a fault. Yet, as their Captain knew, their squadrons would do anything for them.

'Decent flying weather,' Williamson remarked. 'Too good to be lying to a buoy.'

Boyd grinned at the two pilots. Ken Williamson, fine-drawn, imaginative, sensitive and highly intelligent. Lightly built, with mousy hair and grey eyes, he was a pilot of experience and skill. One who never took chances, the complete professional, yet he had nerves of steel. 'Ginger' Hale, though equally as brilliant, was a rugged individual with a tremendous heart. The Captain knew how fortunate he was in having these two.

'You won't be restless for long,' Boyd said quietly. 'The Admiral has asked me to draw up a plan for our squadrons to sink the enemy battle fleet in its own harbour.'

Williamson was silent for a moment, his eyes taking in the details of Alexandria harbour as if he knew his time was rationed.

'Lumley —' Williamson corrected himself — 'Sorry, sir, I mean *Admiral* Lyster had drawn up some plans before the war, hadn't he? When he was Captain of *Glorious*?'

'Yes,' Captain Boyd replied. 'Dudley Pound asked him to do so during the Abyssinian and Munich crises.'

'Where do we fit in, sir?' Hale asked.

'I want you both, independently of each other, to draw up your own plans of attack. I'll submit the one I think the better to Admiral Lumley Lyster.'

There was a moment's silence, then Hale said with a smile, 'Can't be Benghazi, sir. We're off there tomorrow… even the impossible takes a little longer.'

Boyd's eyes twinkled, eyebrows arched as he looked at Williamson.

'Taranto, sir?'

Boyd nodded. 'Come down to my cabin and I'll give you all the dope.' He looked once more about him, sniffed the evening breeze, then strode towards the companionway.

The light above the chart table was hurting his eyes. Lieutenant-Commander Williamson pushed it away irritably: he'd been asking for a shaded bulb for longer than he could remember. It took half an hour to recover one's night vision in this brightness. Lord, he'd be needing his eyes soon! He glanced up at the calendar advertising Scottish whisky; across it *Careless Talk Costs Lives* was scrawled in red.

It was already the 6th of October. Hell's teeth, only a fortnight to go and the final plans hadn't been drawn up yet. Ginger Hale had already submitted his, but he, Williamson, C.O. of 815 Squadron, couldn't make his mind up on one question: what proportion of his strike of Swordfish should be torpedo bombers? Captain Boyd had mentioned a figure of thirty aircraft: fifteen in Hale's range, fifteen in his own. Fifteen Swordfish… how many torpedo droppers?

He pored again over the chart of Taranto, though he already knew the details by heart. He pulled the light closer over his head to avoid the shadow.

He must assume that *all* the enemy fleet were in port. How else could he plan? Trafalgar Day, the 21st of October, had been chosen for the attack. Apart from the significance of Nelson's victory against the European tyrant of the time, the moon would be right on that date. They would need no flares to illuminate their targets.

There were three conditions, Boyd had said: first, an efficient daily reconnaissance of the harbour. Thank God Whiteley and his three 'Maryland' P.R.U.s had arrived in Malta. Squadron Leader 'Ernie' Whiteley was a good hand: operating under trying conditions from Luca airfield — a daily target for the Luftwaffe and Regia Aeronautica — he led his twin-engined Marylands with courage and skill. His task was to keep his aircraft in the air and to take photographs, relying on his superior speed to escape the enemy fighters. Ken felt sorry for the blighters: it was difficult keeping the Stringbags flying. How the devil Whiteley managed without any spares, he couldn't imagine.

The last time Ken had been up to Hal Far, the usual air raid had been in progress. The dusty, pitted field was like a metal merchant's junkyard. Around the perimeter had been dispersed the motley of precious aircraft: two Marylands and the Gladiators *Faith*, *Hope* and *Charity*, now proudly battle-scarred with their tattered fuselages and cullendered wings.

First, then, reliable reconnaissance. Photos from yesterday, the 5th of October, had shown the Italian fleet back in port again after its brush with Cunningham's Med fleet on the 30th of September. The five enemy battleships hadn't moved since, though there was one still absent. Still, five battleships wasn't a bad target.

*If I, Ken Williamson, were the Italian C-in-C., I'd moor my battleships here* — he dug his dividers into the chart behind the Diga di Tarantola, the inner breakwater arm — *and I'd lay a line of anti-submarine and torpedo nets here.* He drew a pencil line running north-north-east from the northern tip of Tarantola.

'That would protect my battle wagons,' he muttered. 'But I'd have to leave my 8-inch cruisers outside.' He scratched the side of his head with the point of the dividers. 'Why not put them behind nets too? Pollock said there was an outer net barrier, with a "gate" into the battleship area. I'll leave the fleet destroyers in the Mar Grande.' He etched in the imaginary outlines of his ships, then stood back to see his handiwork.

What an incredible harbour Taranto was! The ideal naval base.

The mouth of the bay formed the outer harbour and was four and a half miles across; this Mar Grande faced westerly and was protected by two islands: San Pietro (St Peter), the larger, and the islet, San Paola (St Paul).

As a barrier to the swell from the south-westerlies, the enemy had constructed submerged breakwaters between the mainland and Cape Rondinella and the two islands. A large arm, the Diga di San Vito, curved outwards from the southward from Cape San Vito, to complete the barrier to the sea. A gap in the south-west formed the entrance to Mar Grande, and this was protected — as he knew from Whiteley's Maryland reconnaissance and from Intelligence — by anti-aircraft batteries which were manned day and night. *Funny lot, the Italians! Why the devil didn't they use balloons, like we would have? An attack through them would be unpleasant. Probably haven't got enough hydrogen…*

The 6-inch cruisers and the rest of the destroyers would probably be berthed in the Mar Piccolo. He couldn't plan the strike and the targets until the last moment, because he *must* know the exact position of the ships. Presumably, some cruisers would lie at anchor in the Mar Piccolo, while the destroyers went on the wharves, lying — in the Italian fashion — bows to a hauling-off buoy, and sterns to the jetty.

Captain Boyd had mentioned the oil tanks… ah! Here they were, a mile east of the Tarantola. There was the pipeline running down to the harbour, with its Y-shaped fuelling jetties. Yes, and there was the floating dock nearby. *If only there could be a ship in it on Trafalgar Day — what a target!*

Second condition: the torpedo attack must be from the west and towards the moon. There'd be a moon on the 21st. It would rise in the east and be at its zenith around midnight. He'd therefore lead his torpedo bombers in from the west, to silhouette the battleships 'up-moon'. *What about a diversion to the eastward, to distract the enemy's attention from the torpedo bombers' final approach from the west? That's it — the oil depot and, later, the Mar Piccolo… send the bombers in first to play havoc to the eastward…*

The third condition was that *Illustrious* must be south of the Malta-Kýthira line before dark. The aircraft run to the north must be made before moonrise: take-off to be as soon as possible after 2100, and aircraft not to fly more than 400 miles; and, lastly, to fly off and land on in moonlight.

The Captain had allocated fifteen aircraft to each range. Ten torpedo bombers, five bombers? Or eight torpedo and seven bombers? — it was the fleet they were after. But if the diversionary attacks on the oil tanks were not impressive enough, the object of the exercise would be frustrated: ten bombers and five torpedo aircraft? Better compromise and go for eight and seven…

It wasn't going to be a picnic, whichever way you looked at it. Still, it looked, at last, as if their Lordships were going to give the Air Branch a chance. Though Rear Admiral Lumley Lyster had had it planned for so long in his mind, Admiralty would not take it seriously because the Gunnery officers had insisted that pom-pom fire was impassable. *Eagle* had disproved their theory, however: dammit, with her aircraft she had been carrying the can in the Med till the previous month, when *Illustrious* had arrived. Since then, *Illustrious* had already mounted thirteen attacks. Benghazi, a fortnight ago, had been the best so far: they had played old Harry with the shipping and left the port an inferno. It was ironic that the R.A.F. had got the credit. Ken smiled to himself. As long as the enemy was being annoyed and the end of this ghastly business brought nearer, what did it matter who wore the laurels?

Ken glanced at the clock: 2130. God, he was tired; he'd have to go ashore soon to join his squadron on the airstrip. He was driving them hard and didn't want to keep them waiting. They were still a good deal less than perfect at night flying and in night torpedo attacks. Time was getting short: only fifteen days before Trafalgar Day, and they couldn't exercise every night. They'd be at sea some of the time, and routine flying operations (the A/S screens around the fleet) would break up his squadron.

He took a last hurried look at his plans, and then, as he was rolling up the chart, there was a knock on the chart house door.

'Come in.'

He heard the rustle of the blackout screen, and, when the light snapped on again, the Snotty of the Watch stood there, blinking in the bright light.

'Sub-Lieutenant Tanner and Midshipman Brander, sir, reporting on board from Alexandria.'

As the Snotty whipped off his cap he stood aside to introduce the new arrivals. *Good show,* thought Williamson; he was lucky to get another aircrew. He'd heard from Truman that these two were an efficient team. Messed about by 'Shuftie' Kyne, Lofty had hinted. Well, he, Williamson, couldn't stand Kyne at any price, either…

'Good evening. Had a good trip?'

It was Brander who spoke up. 'Yes, thank you, sir.' An amusing-looking cove, with those eyes.

Williamson looked at the taller man behind. 'Tanner, isn't it? Done any night torpedo attacks?'

'Only one, sir.' The chap spoke flatly, a trace of bitterness in his voice.

'Augusta?'

'Yes, sir.' Tanner was tall and wiry, but he affected a nonchalance that so many of them had adopted.

'Had any food?'

'Yes, thank you, sir. The R.A.F. looked after us.'

Williamson grinned. 'Just off there myself. Night torpedo exercises with my squadron.' He watched the gleam in Brander's black eyes. 'L4R is out of commission. Mac's got sandfly fever. Suppose you wouldn't like to take his place? But you're both probably "flakers"...'

Williamson saw Tanner raise his eyebrows imperceptibly as he glanced at his observer.

'We'd like to come, sir.'

'Right. That's fine. We can start off from scratch, then. Better get your gear. Get cracking, I'm late already. I'll hold the boat for you.'

'Aye, aye, sir!'

The two newcomers scrambled through the blackout screen. Williamson paused, nodding to himself. He was smiling as he switched off the light.

# CHAPTER 5

## *Work-up*

6,000 feet and still climbing. Up here, in the loneliness of E5W's cockpit, Bill Tanner had found his thoughts wandering.

'Hey, Brandy! What d'you make of Williamson?' he shouted down the Gosport tube.

'I thought he seemed a good chap. No questions about dissolute youth, for once.' Brandy chuckled.

Bill smiled. 'Reckon Lofty Truman put in a good word for us.'

'Seems so. But we've got to watch out, Bill: we're marked men. Signing off now — the C.O. might want to know our position.'

Bill was alone with his thoughts again. Though the sky was cloudless, flying was difficult, trying to follow the blue dot of Williamson's tail light in L4A. Bill knew the others would be watching their 'new boy' in this leading Vic. He watched the blue light jigging ahead of him, and his thoughts began to wander.

He'd never forget the last few minutes of that investigation in the base at Alex... Even now, up at this height and alone in the darkness, his heart sank at the memory. The Commander had tried to minimise the drama by sitting down, but Bill had felt the thumping of his own heart as he had tried to read the man's thoughts.

'In our opinion Sub-Lieutenant Tanner is guilty of the charge levelled against him.'

The Commander had looked directly at him, but Bill, all colour draining from his face, had resolutely met his gaze. Well, that was the way they repaid you, was it? Kicked you in the teeth after you'd tried your best…

He had barely heard the Commander quietly summing up: 'We find it difficult to reconcile Lieutenant-Commander Kyne's charge and his opinion of the officer with the statement in mitigation submitted by Lieutenant-Commander Truman. After careful consideration we have —' and here he had cleared his throat and raised his voice as he glanced around his audience — 'we have preferred to take the evidence and opinion of Sub-Lieutenant Tanner's Squadron Commander.'

Kyne had coloured. He'd jerked upright and clasped his hands together.

'In view of the high regard in which Lieutenant-Commander Truman holds this *pilot* —' once again the Commander had deliberately glanced at Kyne who, for years, had never sat in a cockpit — 'I have decided to "stand over" the case. Sub-Lieutenant Tanner?'

Bill had stood up.

'Remain behind after I have dismissed the company.' The Commander had nodded as a gentle smile creased his stern face. Bill had tried to smile back, but no words had come.

'Carry on, please, gentlemen.'

There had been grins for Bill from some of the officers as, in silence, they had left the stuffy office. Bill had felt the momentary clasp of Truman's hand on his elbow, and then he'd been alone with the Commander.

'You're lucky, young man,' the man had begun as he led the way through the door to the privacy of his inner office. He had extracted his pipe and begun firming down the tobacco. 'You know I could have court-martialled you?' he had asked, as he stood looking out of the scuttle upon the white buildings of Alexandria dockyard.

'Yes, sir,' Bill had murmured, still numb from the suspense.

'Your courageous action saved you, Tanner,' the Commander had murmured, the lines deeply furrowing his forehead. 'But let me give you a word of advice…'

In the darkness of the night sky, Bill throttled back the Swordfish. The C.O. was levelling up, now that they had reached 7,000 feet. *Course 078 degrees*, the blue light winked. *Speed 95 for twenty minutes.*

He glanced over his shoulder at the other Vics. L4C had just received a raspberry: badly out of station. Well, Bill had held up his end so far, thank heavens: his operational flying was standing him in good stead.

The Base Commander had probed Bill's past. 'I'm trying to find out the cause of your attitude, Tanner,' he'd said. 'I suspect that you resent Lieutenant-Commander Kyne's opinion of you. Am I right?'

Bill had nodded.

'You're a pressed man, I know. Kyne reports that you didn't volunteer with the others in your term?' the older man had persisted. He went on hurriedly, before Bill could reply. 'This, I believe, is one reason why Lieutenant-Commander Kyne is… er, shall we say, slightly prejudiced about you?'

Bill had shrugged his shoulders. 'I suppose so, sir. But I had personal reasons for not volunteering for the Air Branch.'

There had been a long silence then; the Commander had drawn at his pipe and together they'd watched the blue smoke curling upwards, towards the revolving blades of the fan. 'You don't have to tell me, but…'

Then Bill had talked. He trusted this man.

'I'd already volunteered for M.T.B.s, sir. My parents had begged me not to fly.'

The Commander's craggy eyebrows had risen slightly, but he had not interrupted.

'You see, sir,' Bill had continued, 'my father was in the old R.F.C. He was terribly wounded. He has been a physical wreck and caused my mother great difficulties ever since… I promised her…'

He'd been unable to go on for a moment. Then he had forced himself to finish. 'Then, when I found myself press-ganged into the Air Arm, my parents felt I'd… sort of double-crossed them, sir. They didn't say anything, sir. But I knew what my mother…'

He hadn't finished. The Commander had risen from his chair.

'We all have our personal problems,' he'd growled gently. 'What we have to do is to learn to live with them. You mustn't let yours wreck your life, Tanner. Surely you told your parents what had happened — that the choice wasn't yours?'

'Yes, sir, but they can't believe it.'

'Well, my boy, you can do no more. Let me give you some advice.' He'd gulped his drink, then continued: 'Forget the self-pity. Forget Kyne. Now, *Illustrious* is needing one more Swordfish and aircrew. C.-in-C. has asked me to arrange a transfer to *Illustrious.* Would you like to join her?'

Bill had hesitated.

'What about my friends, sir? Can I take my observer?'

'Yes, you may have Brander. But you'd hardly call Kyne a friend, would you? You're better off without him.'

Bill had lowered his eyes.

'I shouldn't take it lightly, young man,' the Commander had concluded. 'That man is determined to prove his point.'

'What's that, sir?'

'That you're no good. It's up to you to show us all that Kyne is wrong. That *we're* right.'

*That we're right...* The words were still echoing in his mind when Brandy called over the Gosport tube: 'One minute to go... stand by to alter course to 078 degrees. Hold your hat on, Bill. Show 'em what we can do...'

As they started their dive down to sea level, Bill felt his worries whirling away in the wind. He could forget Kyne. He had only one real purpose now: to fly, fly, fly. Fly as best he could; train, train until he was efficient. Efficiency meant a hope of survival... for the first time for months, he felt exultation, felt the sheer joy of being master of his machine and job. He had his duty to do and he'd do it as best he could. He forced the stick down, watching the blue light ahead of him, dipping and jinking...

The whine of the struts had increased to a scream as their speed mounted — one hundred and eighty, ninety... two hundred knots... two hundred and five... Ken Williamson was certainly pushing the machines. It was a wonderful feeling, skin-prickling, superb... He watched the needle of the altimeter sliding around the clock: three thousand feet ... two and a half thousand ... one thousand, eight hundred...

*Careful, now — don't dive into the sea... difficult to judge at this speed; can't distinguish sea from horizon.*

He took his eyes off the instrument for a split second...

The blue light ahead of him was suddenly levelling out, Bill eased back the stick, felt the kick of gravity in his stomach. The plane shuddered as it fought the gravitational pull, then suddenly he was skimming the wave tops. The flecks of white horses were kicking up in the freshening breeze.

The C.O. was jinking now and hurling himself from side to side. *Christopher,* Williamson could handle a plane… barely thirty feet from the water and flat out!

Bill kicked at his rudder bar and swung out to port, flinging her about to avoid the imaginary flak. If Ken Williamson could do it, so could he…

'There she is!'

Bill heard Brandy yelling down the Gosport:

'Green two-o. Target!'

Bill searched until his eyes ached, eased the aircraft around until she was lined up on Williamson's blue light. At the same instant two flares catapulted from the C.O.: a green one and a red, arcing into the night, then falling like thistledown. The light dazzled him, and he had to shield his eyes to search for the ship. He saw her then, a dark mass looming up ahead.

He steadied the plane, judged his aim-off and assimilated her silhouette for a brief moment. He deliberately kept his hand off the firing pistol. Torps had set the fish to 'safe' but there was no point in tempting providence… He saw her side above him now, her bow wave a white streak in the darkness. He wrenched back the stick and jerked upwards, clawing for height. At that moment the large illuminated *Affirmative* blinked on at the rear end of the island. The squadron could land on.

Ah! There were the C.O.'s navigation lights, some two hundred feet above him. *Climb slowly, but don't lose speed, or someone will bump into you from astern…* One circuit anti-clockwise, then land on. As they reached five hundred feet, he saw the flight deck landing lights, a blue line glowing beneath their torpedoes. Bill eased into station on the C.O.'s port quarter. He could see on the far side the third member of their sub-flight, so he'd be landing-on third in succession. *Must remember the drill: mustn't forget my arrester wire; release it on landing.*

*Cut my engine when the deck officer crosses his illuminated bats...* 'Go round again if in doubt,' the C.O. had emphasised. 'We can get another aircrew but we can't replace the aircraft.'

He cut back the throttle as the Swordfish ahead began to dip. She dropped away, and then, ahead and beneath him, he saw the weaving lights of the batsman. *Well, here goes...*

Brandy was unusually quiet tonight. Bill grinned to himself as he took her down. Ah! There was the round-down, level with his nose. *Lower the arrester hook. That'll do... steady at that... right! halt her amidships... that's fine! Bit more to port... God, look at Illustrious pitching... Her huge deck must be heaving up and down fifty feet or more. Must keep her above the round-down...*

He throttled up for an instant, felt the sudden surge of power. He was over her deck now... the island was too close to starboard. *Left rudder...* he kicked the bar, throttled right back. The bats waved quickly... port wingtip up, or he'd tear off the wing... *Cut! Cut engine!* He wrenched at the throttle; he heard a metallic singing, then a sudden jolt as the wires groped for his arrester hook. The bats crossed, and he jerked open the throttle as she bumped on to the deck.

*I'm down! My God, I've done it! Now, got to get this crate off the flight deck or I'll hold up the others.*

He waited for the barrier to go down, watched the flight deck officer. Then he taxied slowly forward towards the dark shapes of two Swordfish in the bows. The barrier astern of him would be up again to allow the next aircraft to land on. Normally each aircraft would strike down into the hangar on landing, but not tonight. This was a rehearsal for the real thing, and speed was the vital requirement. They could strike down later.

He saw the ratings crouching to take his wings, glimpsed the C.O. watching him. He approached the other two Swordfish as far as he dared, then cut his engine. The machine spluttered, coughed; suddenly there was no noise except for the rushing of the wind when he climbed from the cockpit. Then the bang and clatter of the next Stringbag landing-on. Williamson was peering up at him.

'Well done, Tanner. Not bad for a sprog. Welcome aboard!'

Bill grinned, glanced at Brandy and jumped down. The steel jolted him. He was on board *Illustrious.*

It was already the 8th of October.

It took Sub-Lieutenant Tanner less than five days to 'sling his hammock'. Everyone went out of their way to make Brandy and him feel settled in. Bill had never known such a sense of purpose, such a feeling of drive and, yes, real happiness, in a ship before.

'All pilots and observers are requested to muster in the ward room.'

He'd heard the 'pipe' over the loudspeakers as he was touring the ship with Brandy. They'd reached the crowded mess decks when the shrill call had summoned them. They hurried back to the mess, which was already filling up. The midday sun was not unpleasant now, for Alexandria was bearable in early October. Bill propped himself against the bulkhead at the back of the ward room. He could see the chart and a large line drawing hanging from an overhead pipe at the other end of the mess. By it, laughing and trying to organise the milling crowd of officers, stood Commander Beale, large and pleasant-faced. Bill couldn't see the chart from here, but there was a buzz of expectation already.

'Where is it?' he asked Brandy quietly. His diminutive observer looked up, winked, then disappeared through the throng.

Bill felt strangely at peace. The officers were a grand bunch, from the Captain downwards. A ship *was* its Captain, and Denis Boyd was respected already. Bill had been officially introduced to him in his cabin the day after the night landing. Instinctively he'd been drawn to the man.

Then there was the Commander (Flying), 'Streamline' Robertson, who'd introduced, and insisted upon, the batsman technique of landing-on aircraft. His method and the crash barriers had cut the landing-on and take-off time by half. The drill demanded discipline. Looking at that finely drawn face, with its hawk-like profile, Bill felt Streamline's strong personality.

The chatter died away, the press of officers parted as through them, bare-headed, strode the sturdy figure of Captain Boyd. He was grim-faced and, unusually for him, did not linger to joke. The company rose to its feet. There was complete silence. Then, as he reached the chart, the Captain's voice called: 'Sit down, please.'

Bill felt a nudge at his elbow: Brandy was back. Bill frowned to shut him up; the Captain had started to speak.

'This, gentlemen, is the moment the Fleet Air Arm has been waiting for since first it was born, but the target has to be kept dead secret. You will, I know, be delighted to hear that Admiral Lumley Lyster has at last obtained permission for us to attack… Gentlemen, this is the general idea for an attack on Leros and, if you think it *is* Leros, you are bigger fools than I thought.' As the Captain's hand slapped the chart in the Taranto area, cheers burst from them all. They were thumping each other on the back, shaking hands; eyes were shining, faces wreathed in grins. Captain Boyd waited for the jubilation to subside.

'Trafalgar Day, the 21st of October, is the day. Conditions are right then — the moon in particular. Now, I'll let your Operations Officer take over.' He sat down and was lost to Bill's view.

Beale climbed to his feet. First he explained to them the major plan of which their operation was to form part. As he reeled off the long list of ships and their task in connection with the guarding of two convoys, one to and one from Malta, some of his audience began to get restive. When, however, he came to Operation Judgement, the plan for the Fleet Air Arm's attack on Taranto, not a sound was to be heard from them.

'C.-in-C. chose the date,' he said, 'for several reasons. First, as Captain Boyd has said, the moon is just right. It rises at 2030 and sets at 0730. It will be at its zenith when you arrive over Taranto, and high enough to silhouette your targets. Second, there remains enough time for you to become efficient at night flying —'

There were yells of protest at this.

'What about the Eagles? Time you chaps learnt…'

'Come off it, Shiner; we were doing this before you were thought of…'

'Third,' Beale went on, raising his voice, 'the moon doesn't rise until you have reached your target from the flying-off position… here.' He pointed to the map hanging up behind him.

Bill craned his neck. He could just see the craggy West Grecian coastline.

'A position forty miles west of Cephalonia.'

Captain Boyd was rising to his feet. He stood next to Beale and took over the tiller. His gaze, with its twinkling blue eyes, ran slowly round the ward room.

'Knowing nothing about flying myself…' Boyd began.

Bill grinned. Good old Denis — what a player! Not only was he a proved seaman but, as some of them knew, he had flown solo as far back as 1912…

'I asked C.-in-C. to agree to this rendezvous. You see, I've flown over Cephalonia myself in earlier days, and it seems an obvious point of return. It's an unmistakable lump of an island. If you fly east from Taranto and then follow the Greek coast down, even *you* can't fail to hit it…'

There was a roar of laughter.

'Of course, I use the word *hit* metaphorically…'

The audience exploded again. Bill grinned at Brandy. Only laughter, he supposed, could make this life bearable. Not long ago there'd been a tragic accident when a Swordfish and its crew had dived into the sea through lack of wind over the deck.

'Find the island of Cephalonia, boys, and you'll find *Illustrious.* We'll be waiting for you — but don't be late, or I'll be after you.' When the laughter had subsided again, the smile left the Captain's rugged face. 'I've asked the Squadron Commanders to work out their own tactics, and they will no doubt let you know them. There will be two strikes, an hour between each.

'C.-in-C., with the remainder of his Force A, will be covering us one hundred miles to the south, in case the Italian fleet are at sea. The whole plan of attack, gentlemen, depends upon the final berths of the Italian fleet in Taranto harbour. We shan't have this information until the R.A.F. reconnaissance on the afternoon of Trafalgar Day. When we know where the battleships are, you are to go in and sink them. It's Drake all over again — Drake's cutting-out expedition on Lord Nelson's day. What could be more appropriate?'

He began to walk through the press of officers, then, suddenly remembering something else, turned back to face his pilots and observers.

'The success of this attack depends upon your teamwork and the efficiency of your night flying. We are going to become one hundred per cent efficient in the next ten days; this means cheerful acceptance of hard training from everyone.

'Lastly, remember this: For twenty years you've been pooh-poohed by the R.A.F. — and what's worse, even by your own service. For twenty years you've been asked to fly the machines that no one else would, or could. You've had the throw-outs, the obsolete crates. Even now they say the Stringbag's obsolescent…'

There was a roar of protest. Bill felt the anger stirring inside him.

'There are many who have flown before you chaps, who flew and gave their lives to prove one thing: that the new concept of naval striking power was the Fleet Air Arm. For twenty years, they've been trying to convince Their Lordships that an aircraft can deliver the goods further, more accurately and at less cost than the big ship with its cannons… Don't laugh, gentlemen; this is true.'

He paused, looking around him.

'You won't believe this, but there are even some who, secretly in their hearts, would not be sorry to see our attack on the enemy fleet in Taranto turn out to be a fiasco. The policy of the gun will then have proved to have been justified.'

There was an angry buzz mounting in the ward room, but the Captain went on:

'So, my merry men, go out and sink the enemy. Justify the past and show the world what you're made of. We need a victory just now.'

Captain Boyd shouldered his way through the press. Bill had never felt like this before, never heard the cheers of inspired men. He looked away, strangely moved. At last he was happy, the shackles broken. He was free, free to prove his worth.

He felt a tug at his arm. 'Come on,' Brandy said quietly. 'Let's go up top.'

# CHAPTER 6

*The Waiting Game*

Though a Midshipman was reputed to be the lowest form of animal life in the Navy, a Lieutenant in the Royal Naval Volunteer (Supplementary) Reserve was a strong challenger to this title.

David Pollock, thirty-four, tall and dark, was a solicitor by profession. Captain Boyd had noticed the acute brain when this junior officer had joined *Illustrious:* Pollock was appointed S.O.O. (2): Assistant to the Staff Officer, Operations on Rear Admiral Lumley Lyster's staff. With his charm, reticence and competence, David Pollock became the friend of his superiors, and it was not long before he was being entrusted with the most secret and important errands.

Pollock had developed a fascination with aerial reconnaissance and photography. An R.A.F. Photographic Interpretation Unit had been formed in Cairo; David knew the key officer there, Flight Lieutenant Jones, who was only too keen to instruct a naval officer in this new science. Pollock was made to buy a stereoscope, and with this instrument learnt to distinguish the most minute detail. A stereoscope gave three dimensions: provided the air photographs had been taken obliquely, the smallest object would 'stand up' out of the photograph.

Pollock had been in on the planning of the attack on Taranto since it had crystallised. He had made it his business, as Intelligence Officer, to keep up to date with the air reconnaissance which the R.A.F., with its Marylands from Malta, was so efficiently providing. But Pollock wanted to see the actual photographs. On the 10th of October, eleven days before Trafalgar Day, when *Illustrious* was refuelling in Alexandria, David Pollock nipped down to Cairo to call upon Jones.

The R.A.F. Flight Lieutenant was busy, frantically piecing together the latest photographs just in from Malta and taken by a Maryland of Whiteley's 431 flight. 'Look at these, Dave,' he grunted over his shoulder. 'Wizard shots of Taranto. Whiteley's boys do damned well, don't they?'

Pollock whistled. The harbour of Taranto was staring up at him, hard and brilliant, from the glossy prints. Fitted together like a kaleidoscope, the map covered the whole table.

'Mind if I have a look?'

'Press on. Excuse me, though, I've got my hands full.'

David pored over the photographs. Through his stereoscope he became fascinated by the incredible detail which stood up so plainly: the picket boat surging through the calm water, its bow wave thrusting outwards at its stem; the lighter alongside that battleship, the derrick moving over the hold, its long shadow casting a thin line across a Veneto's decks. The dots of Italian sailors on the quays, disturbed at their work and gazing up at the approaching aircraft.

He slowly traversed the map, sliding down towards the breakwater of the Diga di Tarantola. An A.A. emplacement (*Wicked-looking swine!*) at the junction with the shore; a small gap in the breakwater; then, carefully sweeping down the arm, he followed the breakwater's curve, its shadow black on the glassy surface of the sea. Suddenly he caught his breath. What the devil was that?

A white dot, just to seaward of the breakwater. Then another blob close to it, like an uncooked sausage… David lifted the stereoscope, checked its focus. He strained his eyes, the better to look… there was no mistaking it. A line of tiny dots followed the curve of the Diga di Tarantola. Then, his eyes knowing what to search for, he saw further lines protecting the battleship anchorage to the westward, just outside the anti-torpedo nets. Another necklace sheltered the oil fuel storage tanks…

'Quick! Come here…'

The Flight Lieutenant confirmed David's suspicion. The enemy had encircled its fleet with the weapon a flier hated most: barrage balloons.

'You're right, David. I'm sure you're right. They're balloons.'

Denis Boyd reached for the telephone. 'Go on. Put me through to C.-in-C.'s office.' He turned again to his S.O.O. (2).· 'David, how the dickens did you get this photograph?'

Pollock hesitated. 'I'm afraid I "borrowed" it, sir, if you know what I mean.'

'Pinched it?'

'Suppose the R.A.F. would call it that, sir. The Flight-Lieutenant took my request to A.O.C., but Air Chief Marshal Longmore said I must stick to the rules. The photographs mustn't leave the library.'

'You'll get court-martialled.'

'Not if I'm not found out, sir,' David said quietly. 'That's why I'm in rather a hurry. I must get back to Cairo and return them before they're missed.'

'You splendid, giddy lunatic…'

Ten minutes later Pollock felt uneasy as he crossed gangway. 'S.O.O., please,' he asked the Officer of the Watch. 'He's expecting me.'

Commander Power was waiting, striding between the bulkheads of the office.

'Well? What's this all about?'

Again the photographs were exhibited.

'Mmm… you may be right.' Power scratched his head. 'Can't see Admiral Cunningham, but you'd better see his Chief of Staff.'

Power led the Very Junior Person into the next flat.

'Come in and hurry up,' a testy shout emerged from the shower of Rear Admiral Algernon Willis's bathroom. 'I'm trying to get ashore for a round of golf with C.-in-C. I'm late already… A tough-looking grey-haired man emerged, dripping wet as he wound a towel round himself. 'What the hell d'you want?'

Five minutes later the Chief of Staff straightened up from the table over which he had been crouching. 'We've had no Intelligence reports of the enemy using balloons, so I'm not entirely convinced. Get back to Cairo, Pollock, and tell the R.A.F. unit to send official confirmation to the Commander-in-Chief.' The Chief of Staff was already disappearing through his cabin door.

Once outside, Pollock breathed again. He ran across the flagship's gangway. *I've alerted them, anyway,* he thought to himself. *They must adjust the plans. Now for Cairo…*

On the 20th of October, ten days later, on the eve of Trafalgar Day, *Illustrious* was at sea, steaming back through the Matapan Channel. She had completed landing-on of the last Swordfish from the Leros strike. The final Swordfish had been struck below; the for'd lift had been raised that night for the last time, and was now flush with the flight deck.

Groups of men could be seen strolling up and down the flight deck, their forms silhouetted against the path of the rising moon. These were the pilots and observers, taking their last constitutional before turning in.

'Well, Brandy, better get some sleep.' Tanner hadn't spoken much. He'd been silent for most of the day, concentrating upon the Leros raid. 'Don't be terribly brave,' Captain Boyd had said. 'I want you all for something much more important.' They'd left Leros in flames. The enemy wouldn't be so keen to leave their aircraft there in the future. Quite a good day. Old *Eagle* had put up a good show too, bless her heart; though, with her shaky boilers, she'd been hard pushed to keep up.

The cruisers had been lucky too. *Ajax* and *York* had bumped into two Italian destroyers. They'd sunk one, and left the other sinking and on fire.

*Don't be terribly brave…*

Those words of Denis Boyd's still echoed in Bill's ears. As if bravery were some sort of tincture to be taken every four hours. He could see Boyd's point: the Stringbags were reserved for tomorrow. Each aircraft below the planned number of fifteen to each strike made the attack more hazardous and decreased the chances of success.

''Night, Brandy.'

'Sleep well.'

Bill craved solitude. Brandy's boisterousness was jarring his nerves tonight. When a man's probable expectation of life was twenty-four hours, he needed a few moments to make his peace with his Maker. There were too many 'bods' up here; he'd stroll through the hangar to check up for the last time on old E5W, then he'd look in on the chapel: *the centre of all our thoughts,* as the Captain had put it. He'd take his communion with the others. The 'Bish' was holding the service at 2115 tonight.

Bill dipped down into the labyrinth of the ship. The smell of fresh paint, the whine of the fans, the prattle of men scurrying through the passages: little things, but they seemed very real tonight.

*God, what a ship! I suppose I'm living through history,* he thought. *Over a thousand men with only one object — to attack the enemy — tomorrow, Trafalgar Day.*

An Ordinary Seaman, fresh-faced, laughing and swinging an empty gash bucket in his hand, stood aside against the bulkhead to let him pass. The man was smiling. 'Good luck tomorrow, sir.'

'Thanks.'

He paused when he reached the door of the after hangar. NO SMOKING stared at him in large red letters. He twisted the lever, and the ponderous steel door swung on its hinges. It clanged shut behind him and he was standing in the hangar.

The cavern swarmed with mechanics. The scene reminded him of the interior of a beehive. Normally a noisy place, tonight there was an unusual hush about the hangar. He sensed the concentration of the devoted service crews, felt the tension… these aircraft were going to be one hundred per cent right for tomorrow. He threaded his way through the gangs of mechanics, past these machines which, when their wings were folded like this in the hangars, reminded him of gigantic wounded moths…

'Evening, sir.'

The Sergeant saluted, then stooped down to pick up a large horseshoe-shaped tank.

‘Good evening, Sergeant. Glad you’re not forgetting that.’

The man grinned. ‘Not after all the bloomin’ sweat of making these long-range reserve tanks, sir. Home-made, but as good as any pusser’s effort…’ere ye are, Tosh…’ and he heaved the tank up and on to the lip of the observer’s cockpit.

The ginger head of a mechanic popped up from the hole, a screwdriver in his hand. ‘Just fixin’ the battery, Sarge…’

‘O.K., drop it. Take this tank.’

Bill watched carefully. These extra petrol tanks gave them another four hours’ flying time. Designed and made by the ship’s staff, yet the air gunner had to be sacrificed; but without these long-range tanks the Swordfish would never get back.

The mechanic was trying to lift the clumsy tank. ‘Cor! It’s heavier than most, Sarge. ’As it been drained?’

‘Yeah. Nobby drained ’em all. Get on with it, for Pete’s sake. We’ve a lot more to fit yet…’

Bill glowed with pride as he stood back to admire his personal flying machine. It was good to have an Eagle here.

Ginger-top disappeared from view, then an oily hand, clutching a long screwdriver, jerked upwards from the cockpit. Bill heard the hiss, saw the blue flash of the spark. He caught the Sergeant as the man leapt backwards from the orange explosion.

A blanket of heat swept over them, and Bill glimpsed a white-faced mechanic jumping from the cockpit. He was threshing with his hands at the flames licking his overalls.

‘Fire! Fire!’

He heard himself shouting, saw the Sergeant running for the crimson extinguisher on the bulkhead. Bill caught the shock-crazed mechanic and rolled him on the deck, smothering the flames… above him he heard the roar of fire.

Crouching and slithering across the steel plating, he ran from the heat. Above the holocaust he heard the wail of the hooters… *Fire! Fire!*

Already the firefighters were on the scene, uncoiling their hoses as they ran. Unnatural, like space-fiction monsters, they approached the inferno engulfing E5W. Foam was spouting from a bell nozzle, but then Bill saw the danger: petrol had spewed out in the explosion, and now the aircraft on each side were ablaze.

*My God! How awful… Taranto?* The thought made his stomach heave — three aircraft less, in under a minute. They'd lose the lot if they didn't buck up; maybe even the ship… already the heat was driving them backwards.

Through the steam, the smoke and the choking fumes, he glimpsed the jerky movements of the firefighters. They were retreating now, beaten back by the inferno.

'Clear the hangar! Turn on the sprinklers! Clear the hangar! Sprinklers, sprinklers…'

He heard the order shouted by the Duty Fire Officer. Then, as he reached the door, he felt the first deluge of water as the sprinklers gushed their fine spray. The mechanic was tumbling through the door. Bill, waiting for him, turned his head.

The hangar was like Dante's Inferno. Orange flames, black smoke and gouts of swirling steam belched upwards from the heart of the holocaust. Along one side of the hangar, he watched a fireman clawing for the emergency escape door. Bill groaned aloud. No aircraft could survive this. *s*

*We may even lose the ship. This'll put the kybosh on Taranto…*

He stumbled through the door and, as he gasped for air, he felt ready hands supporting him. The door clanged shut behind him, and suddenly there was silence.

Captain Boyd felt his heart sink as he groped in the darkness towards Rear Admiral, Air's sea cabin. He was stunned by the catastrophe. What now? What the devil could he say? 'Daddy' Lyster was a great man, a man who looked more fearsome than he was in reality. There were not many men Denis Boyd could tolerate breathing down the back of his neck for long, but Lumley Lyster had become both friend and adviser.

Boyd rapped on the door.

The Admiral had not turned in. He snapped on the light when his Flag Captain entered. The heavily built man with the craggy face lay stretched on top of his bunk, dressed in a dark-blue polo-necked sweater.

'Well, how bad is it?' he barked, his head jerking upwards towards the inferno.

Boyd hesitated. The attack on Taranto had been 'Daddy' Lyster's dreamchild for so long…

'Three aircraft destroyed, sir. The rest unserviceable.'

'My God…' For a full minute Lyster closed his eyes. Then he scrambled from his bunk and reached for his monkey jacket. 'The sprinklers?'

'Yes, sir. Every aircraft is drenched. But the ship is saved.'

Lyster spoke quietly, almost to himself: 'That's the lid on Trafalgar Day. Only the day before, too… Well, Denis —' and he turned his steely eye upon his friend — 'it'll have to be the 30th and 31st then. Can you service the aircraft by then?'

'Should hope so, dammit, though every aircraft will have to be stripped. All the engines and radio equipment are saturated. All the W/T equipment will have to come out and be dried on the upper deck. We're washing down and drying out the hangar now.'

Lumley Lyster gripped his Captain's forearm. 'Don't fash yourself too much, Denis. Your boys will feel it the most. Tell 'em we'll re-assess Judgement; I'll postpone it for ten days. It's half-moon on the night of the 30th of October.' He paused before stepping into the night. 'Tell them to start flare training too. We shall need flare droppers if the visibility is poor, in spite of the half-moon.' He chuckled, and Boyd listened to him talking to himself as he walked towards the bridge: 'What the devil shall I say to Andrew? He won't like this…' He raised his voice as he slipped quietly to the after end of the bridge. 'Officer of the Watch, send my Chief Yeoman to me, please.'

# CHAPTER 7

*Re-assessment*

The flare-dropping training was interrupted by an unexpected development.

On the morning of October 28th 1940, in Alexandria harbour, the Commander-in-Chief's slight figure was striding between the Mediterranean charts which were spread across the bulkheads of his Operations Room in *Warspite.* He had summoned his captains because this was the crisis he had been expecting. The pink signal he held in his hand was from Admiralty:

*Italy is invading Greece. Commence hostilities in accordance with previous instructions.*

Admiral Andrew Cunningham smiled grimly. Thank God he'd won his battle with the politicians. When Their Lordships had been undecided as to whether his Mediterranean fleet should be withdrawn from the Eastern Mediterranean, he had dispatched an *Immediate:*

*My men are imbued with a burning desire to get at the Italian fleet.*

He'd summed up Winston Churchill, the Prime Minister, correctly. The fleet had stayed.

'Good morning, Lumley.'

'Morning, Boyd.'

Though A.B.C.'s voice was high-pitched, he rapped out the words like a pistol shot. The great man was a caged lion this morning. His staff were conspicuous for their distance they kept from the prowling Commander-in-Chief. The only officer intrepid enough to stand near him was his Chief of Staff, Rear Admiral Willis. Denis Boyd grinned; he didn't envy Algy.

'Well, you all know what's happened?' The blue eyes of the Scot flashed round his assembled Captains. 'I'm sailing at dusk. The Italian fleet may poke its nose out from Taranto to cover their invasion of Greece. Of course, gentlemen, you know what this means — our ships are extended beyond their calculated limits. You've got to achieve the impossible.'

He began then to outline his plans. 'Malta reconnaissance yesterday shows these enemy ships in Taranto: five battleships, three 8-inch, six 6-inch cruisers, and innumerable destroyers...'

The bark always softened when he mentioned his first love, Boyd noticed with amusement. A.B.C. had been a destroyer man most of his life: it was in their hard service that he'd learnt his seamanship. Like Nelson, he was first and foremost a seaman. He'd never sailed a boat without winning the damned race.

'If they don't venture out to cover their armies, we'll catch 'em with their pants down at Taranto.'

'Can't get at 'em if they're in the Mar Piccolo,' Lumley growled.

There was a horrible silence, and Boyd smothered a grin.

'Well, we'll sink 'em in the open anchorage, then,' A.B.C. snapped. 'Your torpedo bombers can get amongst 'em there, can't they, Admiral?'

'If they can see their targets, sir. I'm giving them more flare-dropping training tonight. If visibility's low they'll have to drop flares to the eastward of the battleships.'

'I'm sailing at dusk. We've a new war on our hands, gentlemen. We've got to annoy the enemy.' He turned to his Chief of Staff. 'Come on, Algy. Tell us the amended plan based on a Taranto attack for the 30th and 31st of October.'

The C.-in-C. sat down in the vacant chair. Rear Admiral Willis took the pointer from Cunningham's outstretched hand. Boyd felt Lumley nudge him.

'M.B.8 remains the same, gentlemen: the covering of the East and West Malta convoys. Our reinforcements are still expected, but we have now to support and cover our Greek friends.' He tapped the area of the Aegean Sea. 'We must do three things. One: transport forces to Greece to bolster the Greek army. Two: transform Crete, which is now at our disposal, into an advanced and fortified base. You all know what that means: troops, guns, and above all else the construction of airfields.' Then he added quietly: 'Should the Germans decide to aid their allies, gentlemen, the Luftwaffe will be within ten minutes' flying distance of Crete.'

At this a murmur rose from the assembled captains. It was becoming increasingly obvious that ships could not exist in confined waters without adequate air cover.

'Where are the troops coming from?' *Calcutta*'s Captain asked.

'Egypt; that's our third duty. General Wavell has been ordered to halt his advance, to contain the enemy, and to send the rest of his army to Greece. We'll have to take the R.A.F. there also.'

*What a damned shame,* thought Boyd. *Wavell's a genius. Why stop him now, for God's sake? He's rolled up thousands of Italians in less than a month.*

'You've forgotten our fourth duty, Algy,' A.B.C. growled. 'To annoy the enemy fleet.'

They laughed at this. Willis grinned at his Chief. 'I was trying to…'

'Get on with it, Algy. We've little time.'

The Chief of Staff cleared his throat. Resignedly he returned to his chart.

'We've got to get the Greek convoys going: *Aegean, North 6* and *Aegean, South 5. A.N.6* with petrol from Egypt to Greece. *A.S.5*: ships from Greece or Turkey to Alexandria.

'To escort these, we've fitted two new forces into the plans: Force C. Vice-Admiral Light Forces, flying his flag in the cruiser *Orion,* to take R.A.F. stores and personnel to the Piraeus. Then to proceed to the island of Crete to organise the setting up of a naval base in Souda Bay.'

Boyd watched Vice-Admiral Pridham-Wippell. A charming man. Pridham-Wippell, if any man could, would get things moving in Souda Bay.

'Then there's Force B,' the Chief of Staff continued. 'The cruisers, *Ajax* and *Sydney*. They are to take troops, their equipment and guns from Port Said to Souda Bay. *Ajax* is to be guardship and is to assist in mounting the army's Bofors guns until she is relieved by *Calcutta* from Force D. She is then to follow *Sydney*, and rejoin the fleet, Force A.' The Chief of Staff raised his eyebrows. 'Questions?'

'If the Taranto raid has to be postponed yet again, do these movements remain identical?' Rear Admiral (Air) asked. Boyd caught the impatience in his voice. 'And is the 11th of

November, the next suitable moon phase, the final date for our attack on Taranto?'

'Sorry, Lumley. I forgot to mention that,' the Chief of Staff replied. 'The answers to both your questions are "Yes".'

Boyd chuckled. Lumley wouldn't lie down until he'd had his crack at Taranto.

The meeting was ending. A.B.C. strode again to the chart, then faced them. There he stood, undaunted by the fresh disaster he now bore on his shoulders. Resilient, tough, and a born leader, he confronted them, his hands thrust deep into the pockets of his monkey jacket.

'I need hardly remind you, gentlemen,' he said quietly, measuring his words, 'that we must support our allies and our armies to the last ship, even though it's against my judgement as a fighting admiral.' He added, slowly and precisely, 'It takes three years to build a ship. It would take three hundred to rebuild a tradition.'

The fleet proceeded to sea at dusk that night. Covered by Force A, *Illustrious* and *Eagle* slipped through the Matapan Channel. Their Swordfish struck hard at Leros and Rhodes, the enemy's airfields in the Dodecanese. When 815's Squadron Commander had seen the last Swordfish of his flight struck below, he hauled himself up to the bridge to report to Streamline Robertson and Captain Boyd.

'All aircraft except for L4T have returned, sir.'

Boyd turned slowly, his pipe jutting from his mouth. Williamson saw the pain reflected in his Captain's eyes.

'What happened to Charles?' Boyd asked softly.

'Shot down, sir.'

Boyd turned back to watch the bustle on the flight deck. The blue landing lights flicked off.

'I'm sorry, Ken,' Streamline said. 'That prunes our Taranto strike down even further.'

Williamson spoke rapidly. He was not afraid of speaking his mind to his Captain.

'Look here, sir,' he blurted. 'How can I give my squadron flare-dropping training if we're always at sea? We've still got to carry on with the routine A/S patrols. And, dammit, sir, the attack is scheduled for tomorrow…'

Boyd turned patiently to his overwrought Squadron Commander.

'I realise all this, Ken. I've seen the Admiral about it.'

'What'd he say, sir?'

'If the vis is bad tomorrow, we'll postpone again until the 11th of November.'

'We're not efficient yet, sir. I'd prefer…'

Ken Williamson's sentence remained unfinished as away to starboard, from the cruiser line, a vivid orange flash erupted.

Boyd raised his binoculars to his eyes. '*Newcastle*'s hit… poor devils. Look, Streamline, her bow's been blown off.'

For a long interval no word was uttered on the carrier's bridge. Ken felt the wind in his hair, heard the blasts on *Newcastle*'s siren, faint and indistinct across the water: *I have been torpedoed.*

It was Streamline who shattered the shocked silence. 'Destroyers aren't wasting much time.'

Ken peered through the binoculars that the Officer of the Watch handed him. Across the shimmering surface, two sleek silhouettes threshed towards the stricken cruiser. One of them (*Dainty,* wasn't it?) was hurling depth charges from her throwers. The submarine was paying for her impudence.

'Look at *Newcastle*'s bow,' Boyd muttered. 'It's hanging in the breeze. Wish we could stop and help.'

*This is the worst part of it,* Ken thought, *steaming straight past the poor devils. Streamline read his thoughts.*

'It's wretched, isn't it, Ken? But being the primary target, we can't stop.'

Ken looked astern, where *Eagle* followed in the wake. *Illustrious* was swinging to the zigzag now, a white crescent frothing astern. *Eagle* was keeping station faultlessly.

'They're taking Newcastle in tow,' Boyd reported. 'She'll have to steam home stern first, though.'

'Beautiful ships, those town-class cruisers,' Streamline murmured. 'Sweet to look at.'

'And hard-hitting with those six-inch broadsides. Damn shame, though,' Boyd added. 'Yes, Yeoman, what is it?'

'From C.-in-C., sir: *Dainty and Falcon escort Newcastle to Alexandria. Force A proceed in execution of previous orders.*'

Williamson watched the lines creasing Boyd's forehead.

'Has R.A.(A) seen it, Yeoman?'

'Yes, sir.'

'Very good.' Boyd began retreating towards the bridge. 'That's it, then, Commander. We attack Taranto tomorrow.'

'I'm fed up with waiting.'

'You're not the only one, Brandy.'

The aircrew of E4W were waiting in the lee of *Illustrious*'s 'island'. The pilot, Bill Tanner, was stamping his feet. It was perishing here, and the tension of waiting had something to do with the nerves fluttering in his innards.

'How the hell can we operate in this vis., Bill?'

Tanner sniffed the night air. It was cold enough on deck with the carrier working up to full speed. On the horizon he could still see the silhouettes of the battleships. Yesterday's bombing attacks had left them unscathed.

'Williamson is up there now,' he muttered, nodding towards the bridge. 'At least we haven't broken away from the fleet yet.'

'Any moment, though, if we're to reach our flying-off position by 2000.'

The Tannoy crackled above them. 'Listen,' Bill snapped irritably.

The piercing shrillness of a bo'sun's call floated downwind. 'D'ye hear there?' the urgent summons called. 'D'ye hear there?'

Bill felt his heart fluttering as he waited for the order to fly off. The loudspeaker crackled, and then he heard the calm voice he'd begun to recognise above all others:

'This is the Captain speaking. Because of low visibility and our lack of flare-dropping training, I'm afraid I have to tell you that Operation Judgement is once more postponed.'

Bill heard Brandy sigh. 'Thank God,' the Midshipman murmured.

'We'll have another go on the 11th of November,' the Captain continued. 'Armistice Day. After we've finished with him, the date might cause the enemy to stop and think. Meanwhile we'll continue with the fleet to Alex; then to Malta, where our aircrews can get in as much flare-dropping practice as they like.' The voice paused while the message reached every corner of the great ship.

'This is a big operation,' the 'Old Man' continued, 'and preliminary movements will be starting tomorrow. Remember that our efficiency as a fighting unit must not be allowed to flag. We must still carry out our prime duty of protecting the fleet.'

The Tannoy snicked off. Bill glanced at the darkened ships forging their way through the Mediterranean.

'A/S patrols,' muttered Brandy. 'I'm sick of the perishing things.'

The next ten days were filled with feverish activity for the fleet, but for none more than the companies of *Illustrious* and *Eagle.* All leave had been cancelled, the carriers spending every night on flare-dropping training. At last the Squadron Commanders, Williamson and Hale, were able to report to Captain Boyd that they were satisfied — just in time, for on the 4th of November Operation M.B.8 had begun, with the sailing of Convoy A.N.6 to Crete. On the 5th of November, Convoy M.W.3 sailed for Malta, and then on the next night, the 6th, Admiral Cunningham took Force A to sea. Bound for the rendezvous off Pantellaria, the fleet slipped, unnoticed, into the Mediterranean.

The week dragged. As the 11th of November drew nearer, the tension in the carrier became electric. There wasn't an aircrew that didn't wish it was all over. Yet the latest blow had only just fallen. Operation Judgement seemed dogged by disappointment. Now finally this: on the day before the attack, *Eagle* was forced to withdraw. Her petrol supply and boiler feed had been so shaken up by the bombing on the 10th of July that she could not safely put to sea with the fleet. To make up the ever-dwindling numbers of Swordfish, five aircraft and eight complete crews had been transferred from *Eagle* to *Illustrious.*

The 10th of November had held further surprises. Two Swordfish on A/S patrol crashed: the symptoms seemed to have been the same. A coughing, a sudden spluttering, then the silence when the engine cut. A strange business, Lieutenant

'Grubby' Going thought as his aircraft, L5R of 819 Squadron, fanned out on A/S patrol ahead of *Illustrious.* It was 0600 on the 11th of November, the day of the intended Taranto attack. Going was busy working out the drift, for a breeze had sprung up. A good observer left nothing to chance, particularly when he had a 'green' substitute pilot at the controls. As Clifford was Flight Commander, he was too busy preparing his other aircraft for that night.

Those ditchings were coincidental, he mused. Electrical fault, probably — though by the sound of it, the petrol supply might have failed. It had happened to him once.

He leant over the side to get bearings. C.-in-C. in *Warspite,* out to port there... Comforting thought, knowing A.B.C. was at sea with them. Malta must be away to the south-westward, behind the haze now...

Ginger Hale had promised him that this would be his last A/S patrol before the raid. Grubby grinned to himself in the loneliness of his cockpit: at least *he* wasn't going to be left out of it. He had his aircraft; he'd 'booked' Clifford, a top-line pilot. There was no more that Grubby could do to ensure his being on the party... but this week had been an agony of waiting.

He listened to the roar of the Stringbag's engine — sweet enough. He couldn't see *Illustrious,* now some twenty miles away, but there were *Gloucester* and the old *York*, steaming hard to rejoin the fleet. Like toy boats, they seemed, on this blue water.

The Gosport tube wheezed. 'Fifteen hundred feet, sir.'

'Thanks. Alter course to 080 degrees.'

They were bang on position. The fleet (Force A) was trundling along astern of them to reach its noon position, two hundred and fifty miles E.N.E. of Malta. Here Force X, under

V.A.L.F. in *Orion,* would break off and push ahead to enter the Straits of Otranto after dark. Steaming north with Vice-Admiral Pridham-Wippell would be the cruiser *Ajax* and the Australian cruiser *Sydney*. The tribal destroyers, *Nubian* and *Mohawk,* would accompany them. Grubby chuckled to himself. He wouldn't like to be in an Italian ship stumbling upon that lot in the dark.

At noon, Force A would also be altering course to the northward. C.-in-C., in *Warspite*, would lead it to the 1800 position, 85 miles south-west of Zante Island, where *Illustrious* would be detached. Grubby glanced at his watch. Only 0620, blast it… the time would drag like this all day.

Then, suddenly, everything seemed very quiet.

The Gosport tube wheezed: 'Hullo, sir. I think the engine's conked.'

'I was beginning to wonder what the 'orrible 'ush was,' Grubby replied, grinning to himself. This new pilot hadn't ditched before. They were losing height already.

'What's the drill now?' the pilot asked anxiously.

'Well, chum, try gliding towards the fleet: bring her round to 260 degrees.'

So, three minutes later, after Grubby had made his S.O.S., they fell into the sea, pilot and observer clambering out before she sank. They scrambled into their rubber dinghy, and Grubby lit a flare. 'Hope they see the wretched thing,' he fumed, 'on a bright morning like this.'

The pilot wisely remained silent, knowing how Grubby felt. Going would miss the raid now, even if they were picked up: a doubtful chance with that feeble, spluttering glare…

*Gloucester,* however, had seen the fliers' distress signal. Twenty minutes later the clean lines of the cruiser hove alongside.

Her whaler pulled towards them, while *Gloucester* remained zigzagging slowly for fear of U-boat attack. They were hauled into the whaler and then, ten minutes later, the boat was hooked on to the swinging falls. The blocks squealed, the ropes sang, and the whaler was lifting upwards, run up smartly by *Gloucester*'s duty hands.

Mugs of hot coffee were shoved into their fists and, after a rub-down, they were soon seated at breakfast. 'Tubby' Lane, the pilot of *Gloucester*'s Walrus amphibian, was looking after them.

'Does your shag-bat fly, Tubby?' Grubby asked.

''Course it flipping well does,' Lane snorted. 'We can't all be perishing heroes, you know. Someone's got to do the chores.'

'Well, fly me back to *Illustrious*.'

Tubby sat up. 'You mean that?'

''Course.'

'Come and see the Captain, then.'

On *Gloucester*'s bridge the dull routine of watch-keeping continued. Her Captain was still savouring the last dregs of the morning-watch cocoa. He felt tired, though the prospect of today's operation cheered him. He only wished *Gloucester* could have been detailed for the Otranto raid with Pridham-Wippell. And now he had the problem of this pilot they'd picked up. Ah! Here came Lane with the Swordfish's observer. The Lieutenant's hair was still damp from his ditching.

'Good morning, Going. Had a decent breakfast?'

'Yes, sir, and thank you for picking us up.' The observer was stumbling over his syllables. 'Please, sir,' he blurted out, 'we've got to go to Taranto tonight.' He turned to 'Tubby' Lane for support. 'Can you lend us your Walrus, sir, to fly us back to *Illustrious?*'

The Captain was tickled. The way he spoke, the youngster might have been asking permission to attend some desirable cocktail party.

'Will you take him, Lane?'

'Of course, sir.'

'Very well, then. Goodbye.'

Going saluted. He was already halfway down the ladder.

'Thanks a lot, sir.'

'Good luck.' The Captain rubbed the stubble on his chin. These Fleet Air Arm boys had guts.

# CHAPTER 8

## *Fly-Off*

It was 0930 on the 11th of November 1940. Across the port wing of the bridge leant Captain Denis Boyd, enjoying his after-breakfast pipe. He was smiling for the first time that day. The Walrus looked like a floundering cormorant as she clattered down on the empty flight deck, her pusher prop whirling to a standstill. He saw Clifford and Going scrambling through the round hatch in the fuselage. Two minutes later, they were standing before him on the bridge.

'Delighted to see you,' he said. 'How are you?'

Grubby was beaming. 'We're all right, sir. Don't worry about us.'

'I'm not worrying about *you*,' Boyd snapped. 'Where's your perishing aircraft?'

The Captain watched the smile vanishing from Going's face. The observer hadn't given up yet, though…

'I'll take one of the younger one's aircraft, sir.'

Boyd's mouth twitched at the corners. Grubby was a trier.

'Fix it up amongst yourselves,' Boyd said. 'Carry on.'

His eyes softened as he watched the two men disappearing. He'd never known such a ship. Look, dammit, at the spirit of everyone, from seaman boy upwards… today had been disastrous so far, but just look at them…

Going was convinced that contaminated petrol had caused the three engine failures. At 0800 that morning while Going was in *Gloucester*, the Chief had confirmed their suspicions.

There *was* water in the petrol… The cause was immaterial now, whether it was water from the sprinklers during the disastrous fire three weeks ago, or from dubious petrol from the tanker *Toneline* when they'd last refuelled. Streamline had been vigorously checking all sources: he thought one of the motor boats that had refuelled ashore might have discharged its fouled tank into the ship's supply after *Illustrious* had put to sea. There were stringy tendrils of some gluey substance sticking to the sides of the tanks in one of the ditched aircraft that had been recovered, hence the sudden engine failures.

Of one thing Streamline was certain: each aircraft had to drain its petrol system before the fly-off tonight. So, slowly and laboriously, every tank would have to be refuelled by hand through a 'shammy' leather. Only when all twenty-three aircraft had been thus treated could they be allowed to fly off, and time was running out — barely eleven hours now. Even then, they'd be flying six hours for the first time on dubious petrol.

He groaned. As if the agony of waiting wasn't bad enough.

'Sorry I'm late, sir.'

Bill Tanner carefully closed the door of the Operations Room behind him, and the light snicked on again. Ken Williamson was crouching over the chart table, his pilots and observers huddled around him.

''S all right, Bill,' Williamson said. 'Yours was the last to refuel and I told you all to supervise. Come and join the party. We're having a final run-through.'

Bill's spirit lifted within him. He'd been selected; Williamson had chosen him as one of his torpedo bombers. He was being added to the C.O.'s own sub-flight, and would follow him in on the final approach. He was happy now — to hell with Kyne and his opinions. He, Bill Tanner, was good enough to be selected for the Taranto raid, and as one of the Torpedo Boys too. He saw Brandy, serious-faced and silent for once, a notebook in his hand and poring over the chart that detailed the plan for the first strike. The more he could memorise, the better their chances later on.

Bill squeezed in beside Brandy. Their eyes met and Brandy nodded.

'We'll concentrate here on arrival,' Williamson was saying, stabbing at a pencilled circle three miles west of San Pietro Island. 'Height 7,500 feet, time about 2245. 'Schoolie' forecasts we might meet cloud, so keep tight until we reach the dispersal point. We mustn't become separated.'

'And if we do?' asked Kemp.

'My whole object is to allow my six torpedo bombers to approach unobserved from the westward. To achieve this, the enemy's attention must be distracted. That's the job of the four bombers and of the two bomb-and-flare droppers. I shan't detach the flare droppers until I reach this dispersal point with my torpedo bombers.' Williamson was talking quietly now, to emphasise his tactics. 'Only when I see the flares, and only when the targets are illuminated, will I lead in the torpedo bombers. So the answer to Kemp's question is, "Don't start bombing until you see the flares."'

'Could you go through the bombers' targets again, sir?' asked 'Ollie' Patch, the only Royal Marine in the F.A.A. to hold an R.A.F. commission as a Flying Officer. A chuckle ran through the gathering: someone had tied his Royal Marine boots to the fuselage of E5A. 'They'll do more harm than any bomb,' Ollie had remarked.

'Certainly,' the C.O. said. 'Your target, Ollie, is the line of cruisers in the Mar Piccolo. But look, everyone, make a copy of the plan. I've tabulated the targets for you.'

He stood back to allow the observers to make their copies. Bill leant across Brandy and tried to memorise the whole plan, so he'd know of any possible collision factors. It was good to see the Eagles where the 'E' stood out.

Williamson waited with his arms folded. 'All we have to do then is get home,' he added.

'Yes, I'm interested in that part of the exercise,' Janvrin said. 'Would you mind going through it again?'

Bill smiled. Janvrin was not the only married pilot with a family. They all knew that Boyd had insisted upon a certainty of return in the planning; but after a show of this sort, even the island of Cephalonia — barely 230 miles away — would seem a long way off.

'With San Pietro as your point of departure, a course of 125 degrees should hit the northern half of Cephalonia. Fly down its west coast; *Illustrious* will be waiting for us thirty miles off the south-western corner.'

'Same homing drill?' asked Lieutenant Maund.

'Yes. Radar homing beacon at forty miles; and, of course, a searchlight elevated vertically — the same as after our other attacks.'

*Sounds so simple,* Bill thought. At least there was a chance of return if you survived the flak. The Captain was risking his ship to help the returning fliers: Boyd could do no more than that. Bill pushed an unpleasant thought to the back of his mind: Supposing *Illustrious* couldn't make her rendezvous?

Williamson read his mind. 'Should any of you crash, an escape plan has been worked out with our agents ashore. You should make your way to this street, off the Via Carducci…'

'Shouldn't bother about that, sir,' growled Lieutenant Kemp. 'We shan't be taken prisoner.'

Williamson grinned. 'Anyway, they say they'll get us off by submarine if we can make that address. There's an escape pack in each aircraft. Map, rations, compass…'

Laughter greeted this remark. How absurd it all seemed!

'There's an alteration to detail,' Williamson chipped in. 'The courier Swordfish is just in with the Marylands' final reconnaissance from Malta.' He threw the glossy photographs down on the chart table. 'Do you notice anything, my boys?'

The black and white outlines jumped up at Bill. He could easily distinguish the harbours — and there, yes, the larger blobs: the battleships.

'My God, sir,' someone blurted. 'There are *six*…'

'The sixth battleship entered harbour this morning,' Williamson added softly. 'Musso has been most obliging. E4F, will you torpedo her, please?'

A cheer ran through the Operations Room. All Musso's eggs were in one basket! Now the Air Arm could prove itself. Roll on tonight!

The laughter died away as Sub-Lieutenant 'Mac' Macaulay piped up from the back. 'I don't like to mention this, sir, but what about the balloons?'

'Torps has worked the chances out on his slide rule. Using our wingspan and the distance apart of the balloon cables from these photographs, his "form" agrees with mine.'

'What are the odds, sir?' Bill asked, fascinated by these stakes.

'Ten to one against our hitting a balloon cable.'

'Not worth bothering about,' Ollie muttered.

'That's what I reckon. Ignore 'em.'

Bill took a last look at the unpleasant white dots on the photograph. He'd take the C.O.'s advice. Perhaps that was why Williamson was going to lead his squadron in line ahead: if he managed to penetrate those murderous wires, the planes following him should also slip between them…

He glanced at the clock: 1755. Perhaps Williamson had intended to finish now, for he was reaching for his cap. 'The Bish has laid on a short service for those who'd like to take their communion,' he said quietly. 'But before I go, I'd like to impress one thing upon my squadron: I expect each attack to be pressed home regardless.'

Someone opened the door for him.

'Thank you,' Ken said simply. 'See you later.'

'Range Squadrons 815 and 819!'

At 1930 the command trickled through *Illustrious* to reach her nethermost recesses. Streamline Robertson's words released the tension for the thousand souls who had been toiling so long for this moment.

On the carrier's bridge, Captain Boyd strolled over to the wings. Below him stood the Commander (Flying). He was watching the Swordfish emerging from the black rectangle aft in the flight deck. The 'tail-end Charlie' of the First Strike was level with the deck now: E5Q. The handlers swarmed around her, straining and heaving to trundle her to her allotted parking position, which was clearly marked out on the deck. They were unfolding her wings; she looked less like a beetle now, and more like the flying machine she was.

'Well, Streamline,' the Captain said, as he heard Commander (Flying) moving up alongside him. 'I'm having the devil of a job finding enough wind.'

Both men stood watching the bustle on the flight deck below them. This was a historic moment: the first naval torpedo bomber strike in history upon a defended enemy port.

Boyd experienced mixed feelings as he lit his pipe. It seemed so long ago since he and Streamline had whipped the ship into shape during those early days. Streamline, from the first, had promised he'd cut down the fly-off and land-on times. He had succeeded, by means of batsmen and discipline, in reducing them from thirty to ten seconds. Boyd glanced at his watch as the two Squadron Commanders came up to report to Commander (Flying). He smiled to himself as he watched them nonchalantly requesting permission to proceed. Streamline was looking at each of them in turn; both wanted to lead their squadron in the First Strike.

'Better toss for it.'

*How un-alike they are,* Boyd mused as he watched this British procedure. Hale was deliberate, dashing, determined; Williamson quiet, intelligent, ruthless.

'Heads I win,' Hale said quietly.

The silver glinted in the last rays of the sunset. Boyd heard the slap of the coin on the back of Streamline's hand. Williamson chuckled.

'Sorry, Ginger! I'll go first, then.'

The C.O.s saluted, then turned to their Captain.

'Report to the Admiral, then bring all your aircrew to me,' Boyd said. He turned away. These men were the salt of the earth, and he, Captain Denis Boyd, was deliberately sending them to their deaths.

'Course, sir, o-one-o,' the Officer of the Watch called.

'Very good,' the Captain acknowledged. 'Report when she's worked up to twenty-eight knots.'

'Aye, aye, sir. Report at twenty-eight knots.'

Captain Boyd leant over the bridge. He took off his cap and felt the breeze ruffling his hair. He could almost smell the 'flukes' of wind now; he'd had so much experience lately. Tonight, however, he was worried.

The ship's bottom was foul. The weed grew rapidly in the warm waters of the Med., and of course there'd been no time for docking. 'Schoolie', the Met Officer, was right as usual, blast him: surface wind, variable and light airs; upper wind, westerly, 10 knots; eight-tenths thin cloud at 8,000 feet. The moon, the navigator said, was three-quarters full, rising at 2030 and bearing south.

He could feel his great ship trembling as she worked up speed. The Chief must be sitting on the safety valves tonight. He smiled ruefully as he watched his escort straining to keep up. The cruisers strung out across the horizon in line ahead of him — *Gloucester* and *Glasgow,* with their clean lines, and old *Berwick,* the 10,000-ton troop-carrying country-class cruiser. At the far end of the line, too, was *York,* the smaller sister, with six 8-inchers instead of eight, as in the County class. Then, clustered around *Illustrious* and scything through the glassy calm, was the inner screen of destroyers: *Hyperion, Ilex, Hasty* and the tribal, *Mohawk.* A stirring sight they made, threshing white at their stems, their wakes foaming.

Boyd envied them. He remembered his happy days as Captain 'D'.

He glanced at the Chernikeef repeater. Only 22 knots. She'd *have* to make 28. These overloaded Swordfish, with their torpedoes and long-range tanks, would never get off the deck. Williamson, the leader, would have the shortest run. If a competent flier like him couldn't get off, none of the others would. Dare he allow them to try? It was a pity the catapult was kaput…

Boyd's spirit groaned within him as he remembered the two men dead as the result of carrying out his orders. Ogilvie had been a gallant, competent observer. 'In a way it was my fault,' Boyd muttered. Fiercely he watched the plume of steam streaking down the white-painted centre line. He'd have to steel himself again, to force them off by willpower.

'Your aircrew, sir.'

Streamline was saluting. Boyd replaced his cap and faced the cluster of fliers. He looked them over slowly.

'Good luck,' he said. 'I don't want to see you again unless the Italian fleet is sunk.'

He saw the pain in Streamline's eyes, watched the pilots and observers dispersing down the ladders. He turned away, his eyes blurred by tears. *Dear God,* he prayed in his anguish, *bring them all back*. But in his heart he knew there'd be 50% casualties. Out of those forty-two boys, he'd only see twenty-one again.

'Ready to fly off, sir,' Streamline shouted.

'28 knots, sir!' chimed the Officer of the Watch.

'Very good. Tell the Admiral I'm ready to fly off.'

He glanced at the clock: 2015 and dusk already.

'Start up!'

The groups of pilots and observers of the First Strike stubbed out their cigarettes and knocked out their pipes. Silently they left the bridge, having picked up their orders from the Air Operations Room.

Bill tried to force a grin at Brandy, then clattered down the ladders to the flight deck. He felt numb with apprehension, insensitive to feeling. There was no more he could do now. His torpedo — that evil, glistening blue cylinder with its shining 'whisker' — had been 'drop-tested' on to its loading trolley. They'd even persuaded Torps to run off less safety range on the Duplex pistols. After only a few yards running, the warhead would be armed; the torpedo would then explode whenever it ran under a ship or on contact. This was the beauty of the Duplex pistol: a ship's magnetic field would detonate the torpedo. Tonight they were set to run beneath the torpedo nets that screened the battleships.

He paused as he reached the flight deck. This was the last time, perhaps, that he'd register this particular scene: the hustle, the feeling of excitement, the sudden roar as each engine exploded into life. Each aircraft was joining in the chorus, and now he watched his own machine, L4W, coughing and spluttering to start. The engine belched flames. Then, as the cylinders fired and settled down, the flame guards shielded the blue exhausts. He could see his own maintenance crew fussing round 'Aggie', as they called L4W. Nothing had been left to chance. She was as airworthy as she ever would be.

He felt his legs urging him across the steel deck. He could feel the great ship trembling beneath him, and the breeze lightly ruffling his hair as he slipped his flying helmet over his head. There didn't seem much wind tonight.

He glanced at the torpedo nestling beneath the struts of the undercarriage. In the grease that smothered it, some wag had scrawled *Best of luck, Musso* with his finger. Bill grinned as he waited for the mechanic to scramble from the cockpit.

He could see the C.O. in L4A now. He was fastening his Sutton harness, checking his Mae West. What a man! Cool and entirely absorbed now in the business of flying an overloaded aircraft off this floating airfield. Being the leader and the first off, his take-off run would be the shortest. Bill did not envy him. If he couldn't find enough air passing over his wings, he'd dive straight into the sea…

If the C.O. could do it, then, dammit, *he* could.

He grinned at Brander, who was waiting for him, then swung up and on to the main plane.

'Good luck, sir,' the mechanic shouted above the roar. 'Give 'em a kick in the pants from me.'

Bill nodded and tried to force a grin. The maintenance crews had been working non-stop for seventy-two hours. Not only had they to keep the routine flying going, the A/S patrols and the reconnaissance, but they had to arm both these Strikes with meticulous precision, for there was a long flight ahead: the long-range tanks had to be fitted individually, the flares shipped, the bombs armed and fitted, the torpedoes slung; finally, every drop of petrol had today been squeezed through 'shammy' leathers. The maintenance boys were out on their feet.

Bill ran up his engine, felt 'Aggie' shuddering beneath the power of the 690 horses of the air-cooled 9-cylinder Bristol 'Pegasus' radial engine. The after end of the flight deck was now an inferno of noise as the twelve Swordfish roared. Instinctively Bill checked through his running-up drill: *Oil pressure O.K., magneto O.K....* He eased back the throttle and gave the thumbs-up signal to Russell, the Lieutenant-Commander, Flying, and to the Flight Deck Officer who was still awaiting several Swordfish. Bill grew impatient: the plugs would oil up if they had to idle too long. Then he saw L4A taxi-ing to the centre line.

The smoke plume streamed down the central white line. The 'Old Man' could do no more now: *Illustrious* was flat out, steaming into the eye of whatever breeze there was.

From the corner of his eyes, Bill watched the Flight Deck Officer like a lynx. All the First Strike must be ready now, and Russell must have reported to Commander (Flying): a shaded blue *Affirmative* glowed from the wing of the bridge.

Bill felt a lump in his throat — this was the critical moment. If only Williamson could haul that load off the deck!

Suddenly Russell yelled to the crouching maintenance crew: 'Chocks away!' He swung his illuminated bat horizontally above his head.

Bill watched carefully, like a playgoer at some grotesque theatrical production: this was unreal, not of this world. Williamson's front chocks had been whipped away; the crew were scuttling from beneath the main plane; only one remained, stretched flat by the rear wheel and itching to jerk away the final chock.

The light of Russell's bat froze, held vertically above his head.

'Stand by to take off!'

Bill felt his heart bumping. This was the final moment. 'Good luck, Ken,' he prayed, his eyes mesmerised by the speck of light. The pencil beam streaked suddenly downwards.

'Take off!' The handler whipped away the tail chock.

For a moment L4A hung motionless. The blur of her racing propeller had vanished; her wings shuddered as the C.O. revved up to full power. Bill glued his eyes on the black dot of Ken's head. There! The brakes were free… the Swordfish was inching forwards…

Sluggishly, so sickeningly slowly, she rolled forwards. Halfway now and running out of deck. *God, Ken, is that all the power you can manage?* Thirty yards now — not nearly airborne yet. He'd reached the for'd lift already, and still her tail wasn't up properly.

Bill turned his head away. He could watch no longer.

'In position, 270 degrees Kabbo Point forty miles, sir.'

Captain Denis Boyd heard Tosswill's report above the roar from the flight deck. He nodded, satisfied. He could do no more: Streamline had his 28 knots, Lumley and C.-in-C. had their correct flying-off position. Dammit, they ought to be satisfied: so far he'd carried out R.A.(A)'s orders to the letter:

*When detached, Illustrious will adjust course and speed to pass through position X, 270 Kabbo Point 40, at 2000, when course will be altered into wind and speed adjusted to give speed of 30 knots. On completion of flying off first range, course will be altered to 180° to starboard, speed 17 knots and a second alteration of 180° to starboard will be made to pass again through position X at 2100 when course and speed will be adjusted as before.*

*On completion of flying off the second range, Illustrious will alter course to 150°, 17 knots and subsequently to pass through position Y, 270 Kabbo Point 202, at 0100 when course will be altered into wind and speed of 25 knots to be maintained till both ranges have landed on…*

*If enemy forces are encountered during the night, Illustrious is to withdraw, remainder are to engage under C.S.3 (Gloucester). Two destroyers are to be detailed to withdraw with Illustrious.*

He carefully folded the signal and turned back to the port wing of the bridge. He felt Streamline watching him, waiting for the inevitable order. Boyd turned suddenly.

'Fly off!' he ordered.

Commander (Flying) saluted, turned to click on the switch. The reflections from the blue lights of the *Affirmative* gleamed against the paintwork. Boyd felt 'Daddy' Lumley's eyes boring into his back from the Admiral's bridge. It must be as bad for him: he'd dreamt up the whole show…

The Captain turned to watch his pilots wrestling with their aircraft, forty feet below on the flight deck.

'Chocks away! Stand by to take off…' Then down came Russell's illuminated bat. 'Take off!'

Denis Boyd swallowed, praying to his Maker as, mesmerised by the juddering Swordfish, he watched Williamson surge forward on his take-off run. L4A was trundling beneath him now, straight down the centre. Ken was a 'needle' pilot, familiar with the impossible, but tonight Boyd dared not look.

There Ken streaked, tail only just up and twenty yards to go…

Boyd heard the roar as the engine passed beneath him, glimpsed the intentness on Williamson's motionless helmeted head. Her wheels were running level with the round-down: it was now or never. *For God's sake, Ken, lift her…!*

Boyd felt his stomach heave as the Swordfish, its gleaming load tucked between its wheels, dipped suddenly out of sight beneath the carrier's bows.

*Oh, God…* Boyd turned away, sickened by the shock.

Ken had dived straight into the sea, in that short run and no wind, unable to lift his overloaded Swordfish off the deck. Boyd turned to Streamline to cancel the fly-off.

Commander (Flying)'s face was drained of colour, his lips a grim line, his eyes staring forwards. Suddenly he flung his arm out.

Boyd swung round.

L4A was just visible, her undercart flicking the water a hundred yards ahead of the carrier's bows. A sudden flurry of spume flecked the surface as a wheel touched, then Boyd witnessed the incredible: Williamson was gaining height, clawing his way upwards. He was level with the flight deck now.

A long sigh escaped the Captain's lips as he turned back to his Commander (Flying). Streamline was blowing out his cheeks in a long sigh. Both men smiled, then turned back to watch the remainder fly off. L4C next, then L4R… each left the deck a little higher than he last, each with its longer run. Then L4W, Tanner, the new Sub. Boyd felt pleased: in spite of the confidential report which had followed him, this young officer had so far vindicated himself. Ken Williamson had taken him on cheerfully, and the lad seemed happy now that he had gained confidence. There he went! Beautiful take-off. Straight after his predecessors and out into the night to form up on his C.O.

Boyd watched all twelve go, saw the flame float dropped ahead by Williamson to indicate his position while they formed up on him. The flare fluttered, then went out. The First Strike was on its way.

'Start up!'

The Captain heard the Tannoys calling downwind. He breathed a prayer of gratitude. It had been a long hour to wait, but now he was back on his fly-off course. It was 2100 and the turn of the Second Strike.

Boyd leant on the bridge-side, sniffing the wind. Surely there was a little breeze now? He glanced at the anemometer. 7 knots! His spirits soared ridiculously — at least Hale would find it easier to lift off the deck.

'Port ten, steer 310 degrees,' he shouted across to the Officer of the Watch.

The chances for Hale and his boys, Boyd realised, were reckoned to be less than for Williamson's squadron. 815 were bound to stir up trouble; the enemy would be awake, to say the least. Hale would have to lead his boys into a hornet's nest.

The engines were roaring now in that defiant cacophony he liked so well. He watched the flying-off procedure advancing without hitch. Finally Streamline reported, 'Ready to fly off.'

'Fly off!'

First Hale, tail up, engine roaring; no difficulty this time. L5A lifted before reaching the bow, then climbed slowly to port. A flame float poppled ahead by the time the third Swordfish was airborne.

Boyd was satisfied: the weeks of training were paying off.

L5K, E5H, L5B... all followed faultlessly, each taxi-ing to the centre line from their alternate sides before take-off. L5F, with those gallant maniacs, Clifford and Going, was drawing on to the centre line now, following in the wake of L4F who was running down the line. Boyd stiffened. What the devil was that other Stringbag up to?

It was too late for Russell, the Deck Officer, to do anything. The two Stringbags' main planes interlocked. Boyd could see Russell ordering them to cut engines. The Captain turned away, his heart heavy; they were two more aircraft short now. There must be a jinx on Operation Judgement. There'd be only seven in 819's strike. Still, it was better than nothing...

'Captain, sir?' Streamline was calling anxiously.

'Well?'

'Morford's all right, sir. Permission for the fly-off to continue?'

'Granted. But what about Going and Clifford?'

'Fabric is ripped off the lower main plane and three ribs have gone. Aircraft is unserviceable.'

'Cancel L5F's take-off. Grubby will have to miss it, that's all. Hurry — get the other Stringbag away. Hale's waiting.'

Boyd watched Morford trundling down the flight deck, saw him take off and claw after Hale.

'Yeoman,' Boyd ordered quietly. 'Make *Carry on* to the Squadron Commander 819'.

The burly Chief Yeoman of Signals picked up the blue-shaded Aldis and the signal winked through the darkness. An answering 'R' blinked from the sky off their port bow.

'Message received, sir. Time, 2134.'

*They're away now,* thought Boyd, *all except Grubby Going and Clifford.* He smiled sadly. After all their troubles, it was bad luck. A ditching, a flight back in *Gloucester*'s Walrus so as not to miss the show — and now this. Poor old Grubby; his language must be appalling by now.

There was a commotion at the after end of the bridge. It was Going, arguing heatedly with Commander (Flying).

'All right, better see the Captain,' he heard Streamline saying resignedly. A moment later Grubby Going, dishevelled and distraught with pent-up rage, stood with Clifford, his pilot, before their Captain. Both saluted swiftly.

'Lieutenants Going and Clifford have requested to see you, sir,' Streamline snapped.

Boyd nodded. He could see they were angry. 'Well?' he demanded.

'We want to go, sir,' Grubby exploded.

'You can't go, that's all,' Boyd said quietly. 'Your aircraft is unserviceable, and I can't go chasing about after these flukes of wind any longer.' *Poor devils,* he thought; they looked like dejected first-fifteen men, dropped from the side at the last moment.

Grubby's eyes were blazing. 'What are you doing to us, sir?' he blurted angrily. 'The aircraft is already struck below. We can be ready in ten minutes, sir.'

For an instant Boyd hesitated: he couldn't resist such persistence. 'All right,' he said, 'I'll give you ten minutes while I do another circuit. I'll ask the Admiral.'

He took them to Admiral Lyster. They stood impatiently before him.

'You're flying the perishing aircraft. Get cracking!' 'Daddy' Lyster barked gruffly.

Boyd felt happier when he regained the compass platform. Grubby and Clifford had rushed off like dogs with two tails. At 2158, twenty-four minutes late, L5F was airborne. 'Gallant young lunatics,' Boyd muttered to himself in his loneliness, as he brought the ship back on course. 'Off on their own private attack. Dear God, bring them safely back…'

By five minutes past ten, the Captain had checked that all was well: *Illustrious* was once more on course, her screen spread ahead. He strolled to the side of the bridge. There was nothing to do now but wait.

Nothing but wait… Yet there *was* something he could do. In the loneliness of the darkness he took off his cap. He shut his eyes and prayed. For a long moment he leant there, alone with his Maker. Fifty per cent casualties, the Staff had estimated. One aircraft in two. That would be the enemy's doing, but there was also the anxiety of the contaminated petrol. At any moment their engines might cough, splutter and die. They could be falling out of the sky now, spiralling downwards one by one, like autumn leaves…

'Unidentified aircraft, sir, red one-four-o!'

The alarm shattered his thoughts. He sprang to the compass platform.

'Stand by to open fire!' he ordered.

He'd expected this: enemy aircraft patrols, or perhaps torpedo bombers? News of the attack might have leaked…

'Alarm port. Red one-two-o!'

He heard the shouts of the Fire Control, then watched the cupolas of the four-inch high-angle guns swivelling on their mountings. The long barrels pointed up into the night.

'Unidentified aircraft in radar range, sir. Permission to open fire?'

'Open fire!'

Boyd was worried. The alarm had been passed to the rest of his force. Suppose it was one of his boys in trouble? Yet the raider hadn't identified itself. If it was one of theirs, she would not have transmitted, because the only break in W/T silence was to be the one short message *Attack completed.* All other signals, including distress, were forbidden; the position of the carrier must remain concealed.

The guns pounded, the air shook, and then — way up — the shells flashed where they burst. The cruiser screen had joined in too. Boyd felt almost sorry for the lone raider.

A red flare glowed suddenly, to port of the barrage. *Wrong identification.*

'Carry on firing,' Boyd ordered. 'Port twenty.'

The guns continued to engage while he brought the carrier round to comb possible torpedo attacks. Then two green stars fluttered slowly down from the sky, the identification signal for the night.

'Check, check, check!'

*My God, if we've hit one of our own? It must have been close…*

'Starboard ten; bring her into the wind.'

A quarter of an hour later L5Q clattered down on to the flight deck. Streamline was there with Russell and the pilot, Morford, crouching beneath the fuselage. The Captain watched Streamline running from the deck. Soon he was standing beside him on the bridge.

'Morford's raging, sir,' he panted. 'One of the straps of his long-range tanks tore loose. The tank broke away and his engine stopped. He spun a thousand feet before regaining control. He was using his reserve feed first, so he hadn't enough fuel for the trip. The remaining strap was banging on the fuselage like the wrath of doom, so he decided to nurse her back.'

'Any petrol trouble that Morford could see with the others?'

'None so far, sir.'

'Thank you, Commander.'

Boyd turned away. *None so far*… they hadn't switched to their reserve tanks yet. This agonising wait…

He glanced at the clock: 2230. The First Strike couldn't possibly be back before 0200. Three and a half hours' wait, tooling back and forth along this line… and all his aircraft running on risky petrol. He took off his cap and ruffled his hair. Sticking his pipe in his mouth, he crunched the stem. This waiting was hell.

# CHAPTER 9

*The Attack*

Bill Tanner's eyes were aching when finally, at 7,000 feet, the dancing blue light ahead of him broke through the blanket of cloud. From 4,000 feet the squadron had been clawing its way upwards, each Swordfish weaving, surging forwards, then cutting back to stalling speed in the slipstream of the next one ahead.

Despite the effort of dragging the overloaded aircraft upwards, Bill was desperately cold. It was not an ordinary cold, but an all-pervading chill that numbed his whole being. As he levelled off at 7,000 in this strange, terrifying world between life and death, with the cloud stretching beneath him in layers of moonlit fleece, he found his thoughts straying.

He forced himself to concentrate. If he didn't, he'd lose the next ahead. He looked about him, counting slowly: eight Swordfish — but only five that clasped those black, cigar-shaped torpedoes between their wheels. He tried to read their distinguishing numbers: the two flare droppers were still together, but where was the sixth torpedo bomber? Swayne, in L4M, wasn't it? The four bombers were missing altogether.

Bill's mind slowly wrestled with the problem. It did not matter where the bombers were, so long as they waited for the torpedo strike before attacking. He glanced at his watch: no need to use the luminous in this pale light. Fifteen minutes past nine. Only half an hour since take-off? Impossible.

Yet it was true. He'd better settle down and fly his machine. There could be a petrol failure at any moment, and, in this rarefied air, he'd be lucky to pull out of a spin.

It was the bitter cold, more than fear, that set Bill's teeth chattering. Terror of the unknown had been dispelled by those few minutes in *Illustrious*'s chapel. They had knelt there, less than an hour before take-off, in humble acceptance of the destiny God had thrust upon them. In return, He offered them the cup and the bread. Now, up here at 7,000 feet, the question of survival concerned him no longer. What happened to him was decreed by his Maker.

He wondered whether his mother would understand. Dad surely would forgive him now? Though his father was bitter because of his terrible injuries from the First War, he'd be proud of his son now, dead though Bill might be within the hour.

*Wonder how Bright Boy's getting on?* 'Brandy?' he yelled down the Gosport tube. 'You awake?'

A 'raspberry' blared back through the communicating tube.

'Where are we, Vasco?' Bill insisted. 'How long —?' But the question remained unfinished as suddenly, through a gap in the cloud layer, a distant aura of light glowed. It heaved, then died away; mounted again, then remained a bright, glowing beacon, intershot with twinkling sparklers. *Right ahead!*

'Bearing?' he shouted down the tube. He had to wait a moment or two before Brander shouted in reply:

'By my calculations it could be Taranto.'

'Blimey!' Bill glanced at the time: ten forty-five.

Brandy was shouting again. 'Look! There's old Swayne in L4M below us. He's forming up on Kemp in L4K.'

'Good-o. That makes the torpedo boys complete.'

Bill felt the doubts shedding from him as the moment approached. He'd show Kyne what he was made of. After tonight, he'd either be dead or he'd have planted a kipper right up some battle wagon's jackstay. *Come on, Tanner, let's get in amongst 'em…* As the excitement mounted inside him, he saw an 'R' blinking from L4P. Kiggell swung away to starboard, followed by Lamb in L5B.

'Flare droppers are away, Bill.'

'Thanks. Where are we?'

'Bang on line. Five minutes from Cape St Vito.'

'Brandy?'

'Yes?'

'I'm signing off now.'

There was a momentary silence. 'Right-o. Good luck, chum,' called his young observer. Then the tube went dead.

Suddenly the whole sky erupted ahead of them. White, green and red tracer in one cone of flame. Aghast, Bill gripped the stick.

'Here we go,' he muttered. *Good God, look at that…*

He moved the stick forward. 'Aggie' went into a deep dive as he followed the C.O. straight down into the holocaust of flying steel.

The Italian Lieutenant-Commander was proud of his ship. Standing on the bridge of his fleet destroyer, *Fulmine,* he also felt a certain pride in himself. He tilted back his cap. Though the air-raid warnings had been vacillating 'on' and 'off' since dusk, he wasn't going to display fear. Though his officers had donned their steel helmets in accordance with his orders, he, as Captain, could take a certain degree of licence about wearing one.

Yes, he had to admit it, he'd done well in *Nembo,* that old 1927 destroyer. Why else should he have been given command of this beautiful ship? Why should he have been selected to screen the Italian battle fleet, out here in the Mar Grande, the outer harbour of the finest protected port in the world?

'Permission to change the watch, Captain?'

He squared off his cap. 'No, Guiseppe, leave the hands closed up. It can't last much longer. The alert's been on and off since eight-fifteen, and it's ten forty-five now.'

'Thank you, Captain.'

'You're welcome.' He smiled. He had good officers too — though, like all youth, they were impatient.

The shore batteries were opening fire again, down at San Vito and on San Pietro. Couldn't the Army relax tonight? They were a trigger-happy bunch, wasting thousands of rounds on some unsuspecting recce Sunderland, one of those huge, lumbering enemy flying boats. Come to think of it, there'd been fewer snoopers of late. The enemy must have realised that the fleet was impregnable here. The listening posts, the fire control systems, the balloons and the nets saw to that. The nets… thank God the C.-in-C. had seen sense and had not asked them to re-lay them tonight. What was the point, with fleet exercises at dawn? It would be the first time for months that both battle squadrons had exercised together. It was good to see all six battleships in the Mar Grande.

He turned towards the battleships, their upperworks glistening from the moonlight and the glare of the barrage. He could see the H.A. guns of the battle wagons elevated for their fixed barrage.

Two hundred metres from him, *Cavour* lay secured to head and stern moorings. Against the shore, a thousand metres away, lay *Doria,* her more modern sister. On the far side, next to the entrance, he could plainly see *Cesare* outlined against the shore, and the *Duilio,* sister ship to *Doria,* ahead of her. Great vessels, these. Designed by Engineer General Masdea, they could pack a punch with their five turrets, three of them triple.

Between them and the nets and the *Diga di Tarantola* lay the two prides of the fleet: the beautiful new battleships, the *Littorio* and *Veneto.* Thirty-five thousand tons and much larger than their older sisters, they were faster and more efficient. Though but recently commissioned, with their thirty knots they outmatched their British opponents. Nine 380-milimetre guns in three triple mountings, two turrets for'd and one aft; twelve 152s as secondary armament, and twelve 90s as H.A. guns. *What a wonderful sight we'll be tomorrow,* he thought, *out in our* Mare Nostrum*! But I wish they'd cancel the alarm so that we can sleep. Behind these balloons there's no danger from aircraft.*

Any poor devil who tried to fly between those dangling steel cables was welcome to the experience. Idly he counted them. Twenty-seven, encircling the fleet: eleven on shore, sixteen flying from pontoons moored to seaward of Diga di Tarantola and the anti-torpedo nets. A pity that the gale of last week had destroyed sixty of them. He would have felt safer if they could have been replaced but, he understood, the dockyard couldn't produce sufficient hydrogen quickly enough to inflate the envelopes. However, the fleet was safe enough in Taranto, in spite of rumours of enemy torpedo bombers.

Look at those shore batteries, belching their fixed barrages. They must be wasting thousands of rounds, but those impressive cones of fire must surely dissuade any lunatic attacker? Particularly those 'flying onions', as they were called: whirling vortexes of fire curving languidly into the sky. A new invention, and horribly effective.

Yet surely something must be up tonight; why else should there be this curtain of fire — from the small stuff too — red, white and green tracer hose-piping into cones of fire above his head? He reached for his helmet and donned it hurriedly. The thirteen Airphonic stations ringing the port must be pretty touchy tonight. *What time is it? Two minutes past eleven... Santa Maria! What's that?*

He gazed upwards, along the bearing of the floating dock, which was too close to his port beam for his liking. There, drifting slowly downwards from a height of 1500 metres, was a row of brilliant magnesium flares.

'Alarm red nine-o!'

'Stand by to open fire!' He shouted the order as he sprang on to his compass platform. He snatched a quick bearing: first flare, one-seven-o; the one just released, higher and to his left, one-one-o... they were dropping at regular time intervals.

The port was touchy tonight. His ship's company was on edge, trigger-happy after all this waiting.

'Leave it to the soldiers,' he ordered. 'We'll reserve our fire for something we can see.' He glanced at the clock: six minutes past eleven.

A flash split the night in the Mar Piccolo; then another, and another, until the northern shore was alight with bomb explosions. His heart thumped as fear gripped him. Thank God they were attacking the cruisers in the Mar Piccolo and not the battleships...

All hell was let loose now — the H.A. fire was the most intense he'd ever seen. Then, as he gazed northwards, he heard a strange, uneven clatter from behind him. He spun round to catch the sound. *Christos!*

There, jinking and weaving, barely two hundred metres away, a biplane was skimming the water. The roar from her engine now enveloped them, even above the cacophony of fire. She was heading straight towards him, and would pass close down *Fulmine*'s starboard side … and *Cavour* was directly astern.

The battleship was the torpedo bomber's target.

'Alarm right ahead!' he screamed, pointing foolishly. 'Open fire!'

*Fulmine* juddered as she sprang into action. Sheets of flame and lines of tracer streamed from her gun barrels, hosepiping into the crazy plane. He could see the torpedo glistening between its wheels. *Santa Maria,* look at the punishment she was taking…

*Pumph — pumph — pumph!* The pom-poms were barking now. Still the plane came on, now only a hundred metres off. He glimpsed the pilot's head, her blue exhausts. Then suddenly she lifted…

With mesmerised eyes he watched the long, shining torpedo dipping towards the water; saw the splash as it struck the surface. Then the bubbling track streaking down the starboard bow… He heard the roar of the aircraft as it banked steeply to starboard. He forced himself round: the gallant Swordfish was presenting her whole length of underbelly. *Christos!* What a target…

If there was one facet of 'Blood' Scarlett's character that Ken Williamson appreciated, it was his taciturnity. The C.O. of Squadron 815 was not surprised, therefore, when, after receiving from his observer the course for Taranto there was silence for the next two hours. Scarlett never spoke unless he had to.

Then, at 2258, the sky ahead erupted in a colossal firework display: an orange, red and white Brock's Benefit, punctuated by the sparkler effect of shell bursts, and interlaced with streamers of multi-coloured tracer.

The Gosport blared. 'There's Taranto!' Scarlett said.

Williamson smiled. 'Thanks very much,' he said. 'The reception committee seems to be on its toes.'

'Five miles to go.'

'Thanks.'

Height 7,000 feet, speed one hundred knots; bang on course. *Not long now…*

He glanced about him. All around were his fellow pilots; a good bunch. He felt glad to have the Eagles, and Tanner, the only doubtful quantity, was making out. *Except for Ollie and the bombers, they're all with me now that L4M has rejoined*, he thought. *That makes seven torpedo bombers, two flare-and-bomb droppers and four bombers. I ought to have more torpedo bombers — but it's too late now to alter the proportion. Stick to the plan: three torpedo bombers along the north side of Mar Grande, and three with me, L4R, L4C and L4W from the south. Look at that Brock's Benefit ahead! I've lost all advantage of surprise. Our only hope lies in the four bombers creating a diversion in the Mar Piccolo. Then, after the flares are dropped on the far side of the fleet, perhaps we can slink in unobserved?*

'Shall I detach the flare droppers?' Scarlett asked, flat and unemotional.

'Yes, please.'

Ken noticed the gleam of Blood's shaded signal lantern reflecting on the engine cowling: *dash-dash-dot, dash-dash-dash; dash-dash-dot, dash-dash-dash…* An answering blue *dot-dash-dot* from Kiggell in L4P, who then turned away with Lamb in L5B. Lumbering great hawks they looked, as they bore away to starboard. *Good luck, you blighters — light 'em up…*

'We're three and a half miles from San Pietro,' Scarlett called down the Gosport. 'Have you got your bearings?'

'Yes,' answered Ken. There was San Pietro, right ahead, a triangular blob on the silver sea — and to its left the underwater curve of the submerged breakwater. A blip to the right: Isoletto San Paolo. Behind it, the loom of land and the harbour, standing out through the glare. Just like the photographs, except for one thing: the mass of flak crisscrossing and converging over the ships.

'Have you got your bearings, sir?'

'Yes, thank you.'

*Well, here we go! I'm going through that stuff and I'm going to torpedo a battleship. Please, God, protect us. Hold your hat on, Blood! I'll ease the stick forward — here she goes, tail up, nose down, airspeed beginning to move, altimeter creeping back…*

He felt ice cool. This was the calculated risk. No more could be done: it all depended on the skill of each pilot. Each man for himself. He'd better get a hustle on with L4W on his tail, and L4C and L4R close on his port quarter…

The Stringbag was shuddering, nearly standing on her nose: 5,000 feet, one hundred and ninety knots, and still gaining speed. The struts and rigging were screaming now, even above the clatter and banging of the flak. *Hullo, what's this?* A whorl of incandescent light, sailing slowly up to meet him. Straight towards, then passing astern… *Phew!* A flaming onion from that battery just below, at the western tip of San Pietro.

*4,000 feet, speed steady now at two hundred knots…* Would the old girl hold together? Over the island now, the flashes from the guns gliding beneath him. The gleam of the water right ahead — *2,000 feet, 1,500 feet…*

Ken could hear nothing now, deafened by the scream from the rigging and the cacophony of sound. 1,000 feet and still diving steeply. *Take care now, my boy… Don't dive her straight into the 'oggin. Ease back on the stick… Blimey! Look at this!*

Red and blue lines coming up at him. Crawling slowly towards him, straight into the engine, then arcing and whistling suddenly away, behind and ahead of him into the night. A hiss and a crackle and the aircraft jumped. Those invisible, armour-piercing bullets…

*The water's coming at me fast — pull her out now… gently, gently, but with all my strength. 300, 200, 100 feet — she's still not pulling out. God! This is going to be a bit wet. Imagine it – the leader diving straight into the drink!*

*Ah! That's better. She's coming now. My stomach's leaping into my mouth; my head's pressed hard against the armour. Fifty feet — the surface must be there now, black and angry, streaking beneath my wheels. Pity I can't see it. Get her down, boy, another twenty feet…*

*Where are those blasted balloons? Should be coming up at any moment… Look down — search for the pontoons. Can't see the swine. Watch it now, for Pete's sake. Thirty feet —* THIRTY FEET! *I'm thumping well here! Better start jinking — Kick the rudder bar, while you still can, you idiot. Don't let them get you now… You're down. Come round to starboard. Close the eastern shore, then search for your battleship, man. For God's sake, wake up! Where's my blinking battleship?*

*I can't throw her about much more than this or my wingtips will scrape the drink. Hope poor old Blood's O.K. Cripes! Look at the stuff… Why the devil doesn't it hit us? Another flaming onion! Fascinating, really — mesmerises me.*

*Must be through the balloons now. Can't see the brutes in spite of Kiggell's flares. There's the Diga di Tarantola just below. Dear God, I must be through the steel wires. I'm through the balloons — I'm actually through!*

*The breakwater looks like Portland's eastern arm. The flares are doing their stuff. Here come the ships! Here are the targets! To port a bit — now… Yes, that's it — steady, Ken, steady — nearly hit the drink then.*

*I can't see the water… My God, there they are! Three enormous battle wagons. I'll take the middle one, smack in between…*

*Grip the stick. Grip it hard. Stop jinking now. Level up… A perfect target! Five hundred yards now… not close enough! Three hundred yards — how can these destroyers miss me? God! I'm looking right down the barrels of that one — they're throwing everything at me — the whole lot. Steady, then, steady! You're there, boy. Yes — FIRE!*

He squeezed the release lever. The silhouette stood up like a house, directly ahead of him — a huge black ship, with widely spaced, pugnacious vertical funnels.

Ken felt the aircraft lift suddenly beneath him. The fish was on its way. Thank God, it was running true. *Better get out of here. Stamp on the right rudder bar, pull her round to starboard. I'll get behind that floating dock, if this brute of a destroyer will let me… Look at her guns. They must be hitting their own ships.*

*Blast! They're striking me now. She can't miss. It's a hosepipe of stuff… Another second and I'll be stern-on and away. Fifty feet — lift her, man; drag her up and away… Extraordinary how many bullets you can get into the air without actually hitting anybody…*

The engine stopped.

Quite suddenly, the engine was dead. They were falling. A terrible blackness engulfed him. He couldn't breathe.

*Where the hell am I?* he thought. *Thumped my head — can't breathe — I'm UNDER WATER! Better get moving. Kick with my legs — get clear of the cockpit…*

*Is this death? Drowning? Odd. Wonder how Joan will take it, bless her? If I'm in the cockpit I must be about twenty feet down. Hurry, you're choking…*

He tore at the Sutton harness.

*I've come all this way and now I'm drowning. Dammit, why the devil should I drown? Don't panic, chum… Remember that idiot of a Captain 'D'? What was his name? The twerp said I'd never hit anything. The*

*Fleet Air Arm was no good, he said. Well, shucks to him — the fish was running true, anyway. But there's been no explosion tearing apart my guts yet. I've missed…*

*Can't last much longer — lungs are bursting. Thank God there's no hood to open. My Mae West is taking me up fast. Hell, what's all this light, this racket and hail about my head? A-a-ah… air, blessed air at last. I'm alive! Where's Scarlett? He'll be dead, poor blighter. Catapulted out on impact…*

He drew in a draught of air. It was as bright as day. He was mesmerised by the spurts kicking up beside his head and by the whining overhead.

*My God! Bullets! Get to hell out of it…*

The tailplane was still above the surface, so he threshed round to its far side, away from the firing destroyer. *They won't see me here.* He looked up at the rounded fabric silhouetted against the glare.

*Whee-e-e — whee-e-e…*

A couple of rents appeared suddenly in the fabric above his head.

'We'd better get out of here.'

A familiar voice was shouting above the racket, on the far side of the tailplane. *Good grief! Scarlett, in the middle of this holocaust. The gallant fool… Come on, do as he says, strike out for it, away from this inferno of bullets, towards that looming mass of floating dock.*

The racket drew slowly behind them as the waterlogged Swordfish, sandwiched between the two destroyers, still attracted their fire.

'Blood…?' Ken gasped between strokes.

'Yes?'

'Sorry I got you into this rotten awful mess.'

''S all right. We'd better get away from here, though…'

They struck out feverishly. The trail of bullets still pursued them, kicking up the water and whining into the distance.

'Rotten shots,' Scarlett shouted.

'They can't see us now,' Ken shouted back. 'Keep it up, Blood. Only a few yards…'

He felt the barnacles along the dock's side, heard an excited gabbling above his head. A rope plopped in beside them, and a few seconds later they were standing on the slippery deck of the dock.

Ken saw they were surrounded by a gang of rough-looking Italians. The blade of a knife glinted in the shadows. His heart sank.

The men were gabbling excitedly, then suddenly they rushed the fliers. A revolver was jabbed into Ken's ribs.

'Don't resist, Blood,' he gasped. 'They're going to rob us.'

He allowed them to strip him of everything in which he stood. He started shivering, naked in the shadows. Scarlett was laughing behind him.

Ken tried to smile but his teeth were chattering. Scarlett was now standing stark naked too.

A motor boat came chugging alongside them. Ken glimpsed gold braid. Officers gesticulated for the prisoners to enter the boat.

'Come on, Blood. Let's go.'

Three minutes later they were clambering up the jumping ladder of the destroyer. Ken felt ridiculous, standing with water dribbling off him on to the deck. He heard Scarlett panting beside him as a Lieutenant-Commander stepped forward to salute them.

'*Ferito?*' he asked. 'Wounded?'

Ken shook his head. 'Give us some clothes, please.'

'He's trying to apologise, sir,' Scarlett grunted. 'Reckon he's a bit ashamed at our treatment.'

A blanket was thrown round them and they were escorted down to the ward room. A group of officers surrounded them. One of them, a small, unusually fair-haired man, came forward. He spoke in passable French and interpreted for the Captain, who was gabbling excitedly:

'Extremely sorry we shot at you in the water,' he was saying ashamedly. 'We thought another torpedo bomber was coming in through the same place.'

Ken summoned a smile. The man seemed genuine, a decent sort of chap. *Poor blighters,* he thought. *They know they've just shot down an aeroplane. They could see it. They went on shooting at it. Windy types, but some excuse for it tonight.*

'Oh, that's all right,' Ken said. 'It's nothing to us. We're used to this sort of thing.' *Bet they're not,* he thought. Particularly the poor blighters in the ships in the crowded pens — and those ashore, where most of the Italian shells and bullets were still plummeting.

'We saw your torpedo,' the Captain was saying.

'Did it hit?' Ken asked.

'The *Cavour…*'

Ken's heart leapt. He did his best to suppress a smile.

'Well done,' Scarlett said. 'That'll teach 'em to laugh in church. You always had a good eye, Ken.'

'Wish they'd give us a drink,' Ken murmured under his breath. 'Can't stop trembling, blast it. These twerps will think we're windy.'

'Hullo, they're bringing in clothes,' Scarlett said. ''Bout time.'

The small, fair-haired officer was speaking again, slowly in French, and proffering them each a glass of brandy. It went down in one gulp. Ken felt the glow spreading quickly through him. That was better… the trembling was stopping now. *Quick effect,* he thought.

'Thanks.'

The officers left them, except for one swarthy Neapolitan, an unpleasant-looking customer. 'Where have you come from?' he snapped.

*Trying to interrogate us, eh?* thought Ken. *While we're still shocked? Fair enough, I suppose.*

'I'm sorry, I can give you only my name,' said Ken. As laid down by the Geneva Convention, name, rank and number was all a prisoner of war needed to give.

'Name?' the blue-jowled thug demanded, his black eyes smouldering.

'Williamson.'

'Number?'

Ken shook his head. 'Naval officers don't have numbers.'

*'Number?'* screamed the little man.

'Naval officers don't have numbers,' Ken insisted slowly. 'Sorry, chum.' He could not suppress a grin.

Their interrogator swallowed. 'Where d'you come from?'

'Sorry. Can't tell you that.'

The Neapolitan swore. He banged the back of his fist into the palm of his other hand. 'You'd better tell me by tomorrow.' He stamped his foot.

'Sorry, chum. I'm not allowed to.'

Defeated, the interrogator turned to Scarlett. 'And where do *you* come from?' he asked, struggling for control.

Scarlett was as voluble as ever. 'I won't say,' he said gruffly. Not another word could the man get him to utter. Ken was still chuckling when the Captain entered again with some of his officers.

'I am sorry, gentlemen, for the treatment you have received,' he was saying. 'But are you *now* being looked after as you in the Royal Navy would treat a prisoner?'

'Yes, thank you,' said Ken.

But Scarlett was much quicker. In a good cause he was prepared to be lavish with words.

'We generally give 'em beer,' he said.

# CHAPTER 10

*Return Home*

At 5,000 feet, Bill had to pinch himself to be sure he was still conscious. It was Brandy's voice through the Gosport that finally convinced him.

'Thumping good flying, Bill,' the cheery voice shouted. 'Needle, the way you missed those balloon cables.'

Bill grinned in the darkness. His Swordfish's engine was still running happily, but tatters of canvas flapped wildly from the main plane. 'Aggie' was full of holes.

'Never saw 'em,' he shouted. Now that the worst was past, it was up to his observer. Brandy had to find Cephalonia. The glow from Taranto was still visible astern and the flak seemed worse than ever. Poor blighters in the Second Strike: Hale was receiving even more heat than 815 Squadron.

*I wonder what happened to the others,* Bill thought as he checked his instruments. *Speed ninety knots, oil pressure O.K., height 5,000. Hurry up with the course, Brandy. Don't want to miss the carrier after all this.*

*When the C.O. dived at that angle, I thought he'd gone crazy,* he mused. *With no navigation lights and only a blue stern light, I lost him just before the Diga di Tarantola. What a flier that man is! 'Point your aircraft by eye,' he used to say. 'Your eye is best on a moving ship. If you can induce her to turn, you'll always catch her. Get in at her stern, and fire at her bows. You've got her either way. I used to do this from the Courageous in the old days.'*

From the loneliness of his cockpit, he could almost hear the calm words of the C.O. *When I last saw him,* Bill mused, *he was flying like a bat out of hell, straight into a hail of fire…*

'Steer o-three-o. We should sight Cephalonia at about 0100 in this vis.'

'Thanks, Brandy.'

Bill coaxed her round. She was heavier on the rudder than she should be. The petrol was O.K., thank heavens. He'd switched over without mishap to the reserve. *Course 130; speed ninety knots. Illustrious, here we come…! Two hours to go before landing-on, God willing.*

In the solitude of his cockpit it was pleasant to be able to collect himself. His hand was still unsteady, but, apart from that he felt O.K. A pity he hadn't seen his torpedo running, though. He'd felt the release all right, at about four hundred yards from what looked like a Vittorio-class battleship. But in the confusion, because of his concentration in the last seconds, neither he nor Brandy had seen a hit. Disappointing. The fish would run under, anyhow, and would probably show nothing.

He'd seen two explosions on the starboard bow — probably L4Cs and L4Ks. They might have been hits.

Bill had no difficulty in remaining awake. Though the journey must take an hour and a half, his nerves were raw. The blue light of the compass, the stars dancing in the bowl of the night sky above him, and the effort of concentration prevented him from falling asleep. The worry was Brandy's, not his…

Time merged into his thoughts and became meaningless. He strove to push away the terror of loneliness. Supposing, after all this, they missed *Illustrious*? Now that the moon had passed its zenith, it was dark to the eastward. Maybe it would be better to hold on and fly close to Cephalonia? If he flew to the eastward of the carrier, when he turned to look for her, she should be 'up moon'. That was what he'd do.

'Cephalonia ahead!'

Brandy's voice was matter-of-fact, but Bill's heart leapt at the interjection. Then he himself sighted the dark mass sprawling right ahead.

'Another twelve minutes, Bill, then alter course to fly down the coast. Course 160 degrees.'

'Thanks, Brandy.'

Bill glanced at the illuminated clock: fifteen minutes past one. Shouldn't be long now before picking up *Illustrious* or her escort… if they were in position. They might have been forced to withdraw. He pushed the thought to the back of his mind as he watched the coastline grow clearer. *Can't be far off now,* he thought, looking at the white ribbon of surf.

'Look, Brandy! Starboard bow…'

Bill waggled the wings. A vertical pencil of light was stabbing the night sky. Suddenly it disappeared.

'Got it,' Brandy shouted down the voicepipe. 'Steer 2140.'

'Steer 2140.'

Now Bill could not control the trembling of his hands as he reset the compass. *Illustrious* was down there, waiting for them to land on. Land on, that was all that mattered. A hot mug of 'ki', the debriefing, and then to hit the hay. That was all…

'Bill?'

Damn. What did Brandy want now?

'Bill, don't look now, but something's missing.'

'What are you driving at?'

'The undercart's gone.'

Bill felt fear gnawing at him. 'Why the devil didn't you tell me before?'

There was a long silence, then Brandy shouted: 'Reckoned you had enough to worry about.'

*Blast him…*

'What the hell do we do now?'

'Orbit the carrier until we're low on fuel. Then land on.'

'Right.'

Bill sighed in the darkness. So near, yet so far. He'd have to pancake on. Thank God there was a breeze, judging by the frets of white horses below them. Would *Illustrious* wait? It shouldn't take long to burn up the last few gallons: the gauge showed nearly empty already.

'There she is!' Brandy's voice was jubilant as the searchlight beam probed again into the sky, right ahead.

Bill saw a white gash in the sea. He'd brought the aircraft down to 1,500 feet and there — clearly silhouetted against the beam of the setting moon — was etched the dark outline of a 'town-class' cruiser. What a glorious sight! A friendly ship. God be praised, and now for *Illustrious* and home!

Denis Boyd did not stir. Lying fully dressed on the bunk of his sea cabin abaft the bridge, he had been staring with wide-open eyes into the darkness. For an eternity, he'd been waiting in sheer misery for this moment.

'In position "Yorker", sir.' It was the Midshipman of the Watch.

'Very good, Snotty.' He really must get stirring now. He needed all his concentration. 'Tell the Admiral.'

'Aye, aye, sir.'

It was refreshing to feel the wind again. *Illustrious* was working up speed now, ready for the land-on. He searched the horizon with his glasses. Ah! There was the escort, perfectly in station. The cruisers up-moon were sitting targets for any lurking U-boat.

'Radar Office — Bridge?' Boyd heard the tired voice from the Radar Officer.

'Bridge,' the Officer of the Watch replied, leaning over the voicepipe, but Boyd pushed him aside. 'Captain speaking.'

'Echo bearing 332 degrees, range twelve miles. The Radar Officer's on the way up, sir.'

'Very good,' the captain snapped. 'Illuminate vertically, Officer of the Watch. Alter course into the wind. Stop the zigzag. Yeoman?'

'Sir?' a deep voice answered from the shadows.

'Tell the screen I'm about to land on.'

'Aye, aye, sir.'

*Ah! that's better. Something to do at last.* He felt Lumley Lyster's presence by him. *Don't suppose he's slept much, either…*

'Ready to land on, sir. A breeze this time.'

'We'll need it. They'll be full of holes. I'll be on my bridge,' the Admiral grunted, then disappeared.

'Ready to land on, sir.'

It was Streamline.

'Thank you, Commander.'

'Captain, sir?'

The twang of the Canadian accent was pleasant on the ear.

'Yes, Schierbeck? It's them all right?'

'No doubt about it, sir,' the Radar Officer drawled.

'They're coming in fast.'

'Thanks.' Boyd resisted the vital question. 'Keep me informed,' he said.

'Ay, aye, sir.'

The Captain heard the first aircraft even before she identified herself. She was very low, and circling off the starboard bow. Then her recognition lights winked in the sky. The clumsy outline of a Stringbag was wonderful to behold.

'L4C, sir.' Even the Yeoman's voice was unsteady.

Sparke and Neale, then — the second into the torpedo attack. *They would have followed Ken…*

'Land on,' the Captain ordered.

'Aye, aye, sir,' Robertson answered.

The large 'A' glowed at the after end of the bridge. The navigation lights of L4C swung across the stern, then lined up to land on. Boyd strolled to the wings of his bridge; he could count them in from here. The flight deck was ready: the fire and crash parties crouched along the sides, ready to leap into action. 'Haggis' Russell was standing against the wind, his illuminated bats ready, the extra light on his chest glowing brightly.

'Land on!'

Boyd heard Commander (Flying) repeating the order to Russell, saw the deck lights blink on. Then the first Swordfish lumbered in, engine roaring; hovering, gliding, then clattering down on the deck. The arrester wire caught her and slowed her down; the handlers released the hook; the barrier was lowered and Sparke taxied forward. The handlers grabbed her, and the dark mouth of the for'd lift began to swallow her up.

Then another and another: L4P, E4F, L5B. Stacked up now and waiting impatiently to land on. L4L, L4H, E5Q… they were landing on with peacetime precision. Two waiting, but only seven so far. Perhaps Ken had lost his way? Boyd leant over the Radar Office voicepipe.

'Bridge — Radar Office?'

'Radar Office — Bridge.'

'How many aircraft on the scan?'

'Eleven, sir,' Schierbeck answered:

'Thank you.'

Boyd felt uneasy as he glanced at the weather. Low cloud was beginning to haze over the stars at 4,000 feet. He groaned in his misery. It would be too cruel to lose any more through failure to rendezvous…

It looked as if only two aircraft were missing so far: Williamson, unless he was limping home with Ginger Hale's bunch…

'L4W's in trouble, sir,' the Chief Yeoman's voice boomed. 'Undercarriage shot away. Her petrol is exhausted. Requests emergency landing, sir.'

Boyd nodded, then glanced aft. That winking light in the sky must be Tanner's aircraft. *Wonder how he'll make out.* 'Ready, Commander Flying?' he snapped.

'All ready, sir.'

'Tell him to land on.'

Streamline Robertson spoke on the phone to his flight deck officer: 'I've stacked up the others until you've cleared L4W away. Happy?'

'Yes, sir,' Russell replied. 'Crash party's all set.'

'Carry on, then.'

Boyd saw the answering 'R' blinking in the darkness. Already one Swordfish had been damaged landing on, when Kemp had impatiently taxied forward and rammed the aircraft ahead of him. Now another inevitable write-off…

Boyd leant over the wings to watch the drama. *Good God, look at L4W…* Her undercart was hanging by a thread, the whole contraption swinging beneath her fuselage. Only the starboard strut was taking the weight. Tanner would have to be good to land on without killing himself and his observer. Boyd tried to drag his eyes away.

L4W was approaching well. She had dropped down, was levelling off, coming in now, her wings dipping momentarily… mustn't stall … *Tanner, keep her nose up!* Over the round-down now — spasmodic roars from the engine. *(Look at those crash parties crouching in the wings — ready in their asbestos suits). Ah! That was fine — nose up, just abreast the island — tail down, cut back on the throttle.*

Russell's bats weaving in front of the pilot. Then the clatter and screeching of metal as she pancaked; the sparks and her violent slew to port as she tilted over on her port wingtip. Straight for the sea she shot, sparks and flames spurting from the deck. Then silence as the arrester wires held her, poised between the edge of deck and the nets.

Boyd shut his eyes as the flames licked over the fabric. *Poor devils.* He'd liked those two: Brander, irrepressible, a happy youth; Tanner, keen and enthusiastic, in spite of his shyness. Unlucky devils — so near and yet so tragically far…

Boyd forced himself to watch. They'd extricated the pilot, a dazed man as he staggered away from the flaming wreckage. His hands were flailing as they beat out his flaming overalls. The firefighters were trying to hold him back from returning to save his observer. Boyd could see Tanner's face working, even from here…

The foam was now smothering the aircraft — a white blanket of froth. Where was Brander? Cinders in that flaming inferno?

Then he saw two firefighters appear from behind the far side of the fuselage. They carried the slumped body of the observer between them. *Get him to sick bay quick…* The half-crazed Tanner was running towards his observer. The crash party had lifted the smouldering wreckage and, end over end, were toppling it over the side. Boyd breathed again.

Russell was already accepting the next aircraft in. The Captain glanced at the clock: 0237. Time had flown since L4C had clattered on board. Not many to come now. Where was Ken Williamson? *Dear God, let him find us if he's limping home…*

Boyd heard a cough behind him. He turned to see Sparke of L4C, still in his flying rig. He saluted, grinning.

'Sparke, quickly, how did you go in?'

Boyd watched the Sub-Lieutenant. He was bubbling with excitement. He'd gone in through the balloons and come out through the same hole. He'd dropped his fish from seven hundred yards, his target a Cavour. They'd seen an explosion a minute later. The flak had been intense.

'They are a wet lot of so-and-sos, sir,' the pilot concluded.

'Did you see your C.O.?'

'No, sir. Too busy.'

'Thanks. Well done.'

Then Boyd saw the familiar bulk of the C.O. of the Second Strike. Hale was back.

'Ginger, what did you get?'

'Oh, I torpedoed a battleship.'

'How d'you know?'

'I waited to see.'

Boyd smiled. 'Was any of the fire personal?' he asked.

'None, sir.' Hale scratched his head, then grinned. 'Except when I flew over the bow of a cruiser as she pooped off her turret. My fabric's in ribbons.'

'Thanks, Ginger. Any sign of Ken?'

Hale shook his head, saluted, then walked away.

Boyd's heart was heavy. Though the casualties were incredibly light, there were still three missing aircraft:

Williamson and Scarlett, Bayley and Slaughter, Clifford and Going.

The Radar Office voicepipe was calling. Boyd craned over the brass tube. 'Captain…?'

'Radar Officer here, sir. There's another echo on 318 degrees, range nineteen miles.'

'Only one?'

''Fraid so, sir.'

Well, that was better. Only two missing, then. Who the devil would this be? Well, they'd know soon enough. Boyd turned to look at the escort scything through the black water. They'd have to break away soon to rejoin the fleet; it was already twenty to three. They couldn't risk this course much longer. It was incredible that they hadn't been discovered by the Italian patrols.

'L5F identified, sir,' the Yeoman boomed. 'Requests permission to land on.'

'Land on.'

Boyd sighed. So Clifford's and Grubby Going's luck had held after all. They'd gained five minutes on the whole trip: off twenty minutes late, back a quarter of an hour late. *So it was Ken and Bayley, then…*

He watched the final aircraft land on. Wearily he heard Schierbeck's final report: 'Radar scan empty, sir.'

Boyd turned to Tosswill, his navigating officer: 'Course to rejoin the C.-in-C., please, Pilot?'

There was a bustle on the bridge ladder, then Clifford and Grubby were standing in front of him like two excited schoolboys.

'Thank you for the searchlight, sir,' Grubby burst out.

Boyd nodded. 'Did you hit anything?'

'Cruiser, sir. In the Mar Piccolo.'

'How d'you know?'

'We had an argument about it, sir; we're sure we hit her.'

Boyd dismissed them. They hadn't missed the party, after all. Amazing, he thought, that the pilots all looked at it like that — as a party. He knew they had already asked if they could repeat the raid next day. Impossible, but what a spirit it showed. He turned; the Navigating Officer was speaking from the compass platform.

'Course to rejoin C.-in-C., sir, 192 degrees.'

'Bring her round, Pilot,' Boyd ordered quietly. 'Reduce speed to twenty-two knots.'

# CHAPTER 11

## *Retribution*

At first light on the 10th of January 1941, *Illustrious* was nosing her way through the Pantellaria channel. From the carrier's bridge the sandy wedge of the island glowed golden in the dawn.

*A beautiful sight,* thought Bill Tanner. Yet now, from where he stood on the 'goofers' (the unofficial observation platform), he could feel the tension on the bridge. The Captain strolled restlessly to and fro, eyes alert, pipe jammed in mouth. Ahead, the smudges of the eastbound merchant ships from Gibraltar were showing over the horizon. *Warspite* was flashing now; a string of bunting streamed suddenly from the flagship's yardarm. *We'll turn at any moment,* thought Bill. *Here we go…*

The great ship heeled to her rudder as the fleet turned in succession, back to their original course for Malta.

Bill had recently landed from his own dawn patrol in Swordfish L4Y. He and Brandy were revelling in the warmth of this January sun, but they could not relax. The enemy could pounce at any moment from Sicily, less than seventy miles away. The German Fliegerkorps X had transferred from Norway to Sicily.

'How many of the Luftwaffe were in Catania and Comiso, did the Captain say?' asked Brandy quietly.

'Hundreds,' Bill replied. 'Heinkel 113s, Junkers 88s…'

'And the Stukas?'

'Yes, the Ju 87s. Hitler's got it in for Musso.'

Brandy whistled. 'And us, judging by the shadowers we've had since dawn.'

Bill nodded. The morning had been busy already with continuous A/S and fighter patrols over the fleet. Charles Evans and his fighter boys had been busy while the Swordfish bombers did their stuff.

'D'you reckon Jago got that ship, Brandy?' Bill asked.

'Sure — his bombs went through the funnel.'

'A good hand, the new C.O.,' Bill said. 'Reckon he's the best replacement we could have since Ken's gone.'

'Reckon so,' the observer said quietly. 'He's a driver all right. We've another strike at noon.'

Bill looked at his watch: five to twelve. His stomach sank; he still got the willies before any operation.

'Brandy?'

'Yep?'

'D'you reckon we did all right in the Taranto raid?' Bill looked carefully at his observer.

Brandy swung towards him. ''Course. Why d'you ask? Someone's got to miss, y'know.'

Bill shrugged his shoulders. 'Oh, I dunno. Just that I can picture Kyne laughing like a drain when he reads the reports.'

'Stop fussing, for Pete's sake,' Brandy said angrily. 'We did our best. We've helped to put the Italian fleet out of action for two months.'

'I can't remember what the exact score was,' Bill said.

'A Littorio and two Cavour battleships put out of action and two cruisers damaged; not forgetting that their seaplane base and a third of their oil production were destroyed.'

'Come on,' Brandy said. 'We'd better get down to the hangar or the C.O.'ll be nattering... my God, Bill! Look at those!'

As Bill peered in the direction of Brandy's outstretched arm, the alarm blared behind them.

'Alarm starboard, green two-o!'

Bill saw the Captain bending over the voicepipe.

'Starboard twenty,' Boyd commanded. 'Open fire!'

The fire gongs tinged from the directors. The 4.5s opened up. Seconds later the pom-poms began pounding rhythmically.

'I'm going below,' Brandy shouted. 'Meet you in the hangar.'

Bill took a last look at the approaching torpedo bombers: two Italian 8.79s, and *Illustrious* was lumbering straight towards them. She was beginning to swing now... Ah! there went the fish!

With a professional eye Bill admired the precision of the enemy pilots. The torpedoes dropped within a second of each other. Bill saw both splashes, then watched the S.79s lift and turn away. They bore charmed lives in the middle of that stuff. The language of the gunner from S.3 pom-pom was as blistering as his gun barrels.

As the Captain crouched over the voicepipe, his tin hat fell over his eyes. He tore it off, then, seeing Bill, tossed it towards him. 'Port ten... steady...'

Bill held his breath. He watched the lines of foaming bubbles slithering down either side of the great ship as she combed the tracks. There was a deafening roar and the first of Evans's five Fulmars came streaking by, hell-bent after the torpedo bombers. The fighters had been short of fuel, and were coming in to land as soon as the other six Fulmars, already ranged and starting up, had taken off.

There streaked the first of Evans's second patrol of fighters! Its first Fulmar was airborne.

It was at this moment that Bill was surprised to see the Captain spin round, peering upwards into the sun. His face wore an expression of horror.

Hans Siebling was a veteran of twenty, a Pilot Officer in Fliegerkorps X, Hitler's Tenth Air Corps. The transfer to the sun of Sicily had come as a pleasant surprise for him, after the chill of Norway. He grinned as he snapped shut the hood of his Junkers 87, giving the thumbs-up signal to his mechanic and opening the throttle. His ugly aircraft lumbered forward and gathered speed.

He felt the Stuka lift ponderously from the ground; with her 3,000-kg bomb and full tanks, the dive-bomber was sluggish at this stage of the flight. He looked in his mirror; the others were following with mechanical precision. He'd take her up to two thousand feet and circuit until his whole force was in formation: over two hundred Stukas, bombers and twin-engined fighters. The sky was black with aircraft; three hundred and fifty had come from Norway.

The pilots knew their targets by heart: Malta, the British base that refused to surrender. That yellow heap of sandstone from which their submarines operated and their aircraft flew; and, of course, the aircraft carrier *Illustrious.* Hans grinned. They were after her now. They had her taped. Pantellaria had sighted her at dawn. Thirty minutes should see it all over...

He looked up. It was grand to see the Messerschmitt 110s weaving overhead. He checked on his sub-flight: good, Johann and Kurt were there on either side and a few metres above him.

Cape Passaro slid away beneath him, and then they were above the Sicilian channel. He looked over the side. How the devil did the British submarines slip through that minefield?

Now he could pick out Malta and Gozo, away to port. Ah! There was Pantellaria right ahead — a yellow wedge of barren sandstone. If the Italians could hold it, it must be impregnable.

*'Achtung! Illustrious…'*

Hans heard the leader's alert over the short-wave radio. He looked through the Perspex nose of his aircraft. *Himmel!* The whole British fleet was out — look, there was the carrier, hauled out of line. Flying off fighters, perhaps? The M.E.s would deal with them.

*Are you ready, Hans? Bomb safety lever OFF? Sight cleared? She's coming within range; I can see her plainly now… A huge rectangular flight deck with its two lift wells.* A fighter was taking off; he could see it crawling like an insect along the flight deck, along the plume of steam wisping down the centre line. *I'd better hurry,* he thought, *or we'll be bounced…*

*'Achtung!'*

He heard his voice, triumphant and confident. They'd rehearsed this so often. *Don't rush things, Hans, that's always been your trouble. Wait until everything is set. Wait until you see the Italian torpedo bombers drawing off the Fulmars. Then, from either bow and from the starboard quarter, peel off from out of the sun.*

*Work round more into the sun… a few more seconds* … Where were the damned Italians? They should be running in now — ah! Those were torpedo tracks, weren't they? Yes, he could see the S.79S now, legging it hell for leather for Sicily and smothered by shell-bursts. There streaked the Fulmars after them.

'Hold your hats on! Here we go!'

His heart came into his mouth as he pushed her nose down. Ungainly the Stuka might be in level flight, but *boy, you watch her now,* he thought…

He felt the force of gravity beginning to press him against his seat, saw Johann and Kurt peeling off on either side. He was vertical now and going down fast. He switched on the siren, but couldn't hear it for the racket and the scream of the wind.

They were flinging everything up at him now. Black puffs, flashing orange as he hurtled downwards — must be their A.A. armament. There she was, a great grey slab rushing up to meet him. Where were the pom-pom mountings, his own special target?

The carrier was jumping up at him now, whirling into focus. There were her starboard pom-poms, forward of the bridge. He could see the crew, tin-hatted marionettes, feeding the belts into the leaping barrels. *Three hundred metres, two hundred… hold her steady now, Hans, grip the stick, you're almost there. Kill the swine… don't miss now. Hold on, hold on, hold on…* His eardrums were bursting, his nerves screaming. *Don't fail now, don't fail, hold on. Now!*

He squeezed the bomb release. Gently he allowed the stick to come forward, then pulled out. The pom-pom streaked beneath his wheels. The white faces of the crew were gazing upwards grimly; they were still firing their guns.

*Careful, not too fast… steady, or you'll black out.* He flung her over on her side to watch his bomb. There it was… a great black thing, toppling down on the upturned faces…

'Stukas! Green two-o, Red three-o. Green one-two…'

When Captain Boyd heard the alarm he knew that this was their testing time. This was the moment he'd been dreading for so long. Since Taranto, he'd known that the Germans would repay with interest one day. The bombardments of Valona on December 10th, and of Bardia on January 3rd, had stung the enemy to fury.

When the first radar reports had come in a few minutes ago, he'd known the Stukas were on their way. Intelligence was seldom in error: there were over five hundred of Hitler's First XI waiting in Sicily. They'd been boasting long enough that they'd get *Illustrious,* dammit…

'Open fire!'

*I'll have to risk the fighters,* he thought, as he heard Evans's Fulmars roaring down the flight deck. *They'll scramble off somehow. Hurry up, for God's sake, I shall want to throw the ship about to miss them — Christopher! Look at that!*

He raised his arm to search up-sun. Squinting with one eye, and shading it with the palm of his hand, he peered into the blinding light. Out of the sky hurtled three black shapes, in clover-leaf formation, and growing larger at every second. They had already peeled off and were diving vertically now. God, they were brave men…

Five hundred feet, four hundred… the noise was terrifying. They'd switched on the sirens and their banshee wails, but they'd need more than that.

*By God, they're giving it us, too,* he thought. At masthead height, the leader pulled out. Boyd could see the pilot's head, motionless in concentration as he roared with a nerve-racking scream over the bow. He heard the shuddering of the air brakes, saw the thousand-pounder dropping, toppling like a stone… it would land on the flight deck. A great black monster, the size of a Baby Austin… Boyd groaned as the ship shuddered from the impact. The bomb had hit P1, the port pom-pom. He could see the flash and the orange flame. Slowly the smoke cleared. The sickening shambles was too awful to look upon…

Then another and another… Down the Stukas came, wave after wave through the shell-bursts. Boyd saw the second wave poised to attack, as the last of the Fulmars was taking off through the splashes. *Now I can manoeuvre my* ship, he thought. *Thank God I'm clear of the fleet.*

'Hard-a-starboard!'

He waited while the second wave peeled off. Stacked up in layers, the Stukas waited their turn as if on a peacetime air display. Then, three by three, they peeled off. Their noses went down, their tails came up.

'Midships — hard-a-port!'

The second wave was overhead now. *Yes, pulling out — look at their perishing black crosses... Dammit, that pilot is waving... Look! He's even below me, below the level of the flight deck...*

Again and again he felt his ship struck. She reeled from the blows, trembling from her hurts. S2, with poor old Austin, was wrecked. S1 pom-pom was also hit. The swine were going for the guns. When the armament had ceased firing, the bombers would take their time to finish her off...

God, the Fulmars were slow! Hadn't they got up there, even yet? Poor old Evans, he was doing his best, dammit. The Air Arm had always to put up with second-rate machines.

The third wave was hurtling down now, on either quarter.

'Hard-a-port!' He gripped the voicepipe, fear groping at his vitals as he listened to the Stukas screaming downwards. He saw them dive to deck level, then pull out. The bombs continued to rain.

A tremendous shock, a cloud of smoke and flame as the bomb went through the armoured flight deck. The after lift jumped. It came up through the deck and landed on its side inside the well. There'd been a pilot there, waiting, sitting in his cockpit... Boyd looked away.

*God, look at the next lot! High-level as well as the Stukas. Better watch the high-level. More time to dodge. Can't do much about the Stukas anyway.*

'Keep firing, lads, keep the beggars up,' he shouted. He saw Guns, grim-faced and intent, peering upwards from the director. Then down hurtled the Stukas, their banshee sirens wailing hideously.

'Midships — steady—'

'Steady, sir.'

'Hard-a-starboard!'

The bomb crashed down and pierced the flight deck. Boyd steeled himself from ducking, yet strangely felt no fear now. *What are they doing to my beautiful ship?* he asked himself angrily. *That bomb must have gone through the Boys' mess deck. I can see the sea through those holes... wonder if she's damaged below the waterline? Hullo... what's that pilot doing there? Oh, of course, I gave him my tin hat...*

'Tanner,' he shouted. 'Give me my hat.'

The pilot stepped forward. He was pale, but he grinned as he saluted.

'Go below and see what's happened to the after 4.5s,' said Boyd. 'They've stopped firing.'

'Aye, aye, sir.' The lad was saluting as if he was on the quarterdeck.

'Then come back and report. Look out! Here comes another swine!'

Bill Tanner had to steel himself to advance any further. The sights he had passed on the way down to the hangar had made him physically sick. Never before had he seen what battle conditions were like. He forced himself onwards through the stench, the smoke and the holocaust. There was another ear-splitting crack and the great ship jumped once more: it felt like the after lift well all over again.

Down here in the darkness, terror gripped him. He slithered gingerly along the passage, his feet groping in the blackness for the jagged abyss blasted by a bomb. Twice his feet prodded the softness of a dead man, and he passed on, unable to help. It was a pity the secondary lighting was out as well. He bumped into Commander Tuck who, with Mr Gutteridge, the tireless shipwright, was frenziedly trying to cut a hole in the side of the hangar.

'Lend us a hand, Tanner.'

The demand for physical exertion suddenly helped. He picked up a crowbar and attacked the metal.

'Can't get into the hangar, Bill,' Gutteridge gasped. 'Take a look. This hole's to drain off what's in there.'

Bill peered through the jagged hole. The hangar was ablaze from end to end, the fires fanned by the gaping hole of the twisted forward lift. The wind was rushing in, and the flames licked along to the after lift, which had been blown end-on in its well. The sprinklers had been turned on, but the water lines had been wrecked by a thousand-pounder. Water and petrol now slopped two feet deep about the enormous cavity. With this surging weight loose inside her, the ship's stability was endangered, and she had taken on a dangerous list. Much more of this and she might roll over. This realisation added desperation to the efforts of the damage control party.

Tuck was magnificent: supremely efficient at his job, he was quite unflurried in the emergency. Now he stood up. The hole was finished, down to deck level. He and his men could do no more. Then suddenly, as the ship rolled, water began to rush through the hole. Bill watched it pour in a torrent down the passage, down to the scuppers and away. *Better push on; the Captain'll be waiting.* Bill left them and continued his journey aft, passing through what once had been the galley.

By one of the stoves he found the First Lieutenant crouching over a mortally wounded man. Rosy Baker looked up. 'I've given him a double dose of morphia by mistake, Tanner. Ask the doc what I should do if you see him, will you?'

Bill nodded: the poor fellow would sleep all the better. Bill floundered onwards, crossing to the port passage. He stumbled upon Grubby Going hauling on a fire hose.

'Thanks, Bill. The After Damage Control Officer's been killed, so I'm doing his job. Go aft, chum: they're in a hell of a mess down there. The A.A. ammunition hoists are blazing.'

Bill started slithering aft. He had gone thirty feet and turned the corner by the wrecked ward room, when there was a blinding flash and he found himself lying spread-eagled on the deck. He picked himself up, his senses reeling. *God! That must have gone through where Grubby had been standing…*

Bill retraced his steps and groped forwards again, on his hands and knees in the darkness. Then he felt the wetness of a fire hose. He followed this, feeling his way along it in the blackness. Suddenly it dipped down into the void of the deck below.

Nothing, except for the roar of flames and a rushing wind.

'Grubby, you O.K.?'

There was no answer.

Bill grasped the hose and gingerly lowered himself into the abyss. His feet touched the corticene of the deck below, but nothing moved; there was no sign of life.

Once more Bill started his pilgrimage towards the after gun bays… couldn't be far off now. Then, in the choking fumes, he ran across Mr Howe, the Warrant Officer whose station was at the after ammunition supply.

'Where's Going?' Howe shouted. 'He ordered me to get to hell out of here.'

'Last bomb got him, I think,' Bill called back. 'Obey his orders or you'll be trapped.' He nodded at the plume of flame slicking along the bulkhead, a stream of flaming petrol that roared and hissed like a giant's blowlamp.

Mr Howe took his party of seamen with him and stumbled away from the inferno. 'Hoists are getting hot,' he shouted. 'Tell the Captain: getting near the magazines.'

*If that lot goes up...*

Bill stumbled onwards, then suddenly came upon the shambles that had been the gun bay of a port 4.5. In the smoke and darkness he caught sight of a flickering torch and the outline of stretcher-bearers. The groans of the dying mingled with the roar of flames from the hanger. Then, from somewhere ahead, came the distant thumping of the guns. *We're still hitting back, anyway,* Bill thought, *but there's nothing anyone can do down here. Better get back and tell the Captain. Easiest along the flight deck — to hell with these bombs. I'll reach the quarterdeck and climb up from there.*

He could scarcely recognise the place. Here, away from the immediate danger of the fires, they had brought the wounded and the dying. They lay in rows, the surgeons and their attendants passing from casualty to casualty as the stretcher-bearers staggered in with their pathetic loads.

Bill found a ladder and started climbing. On the hangar deck he bumped into the Gunner.

'Where're you going, Tanner?' Bill Banham gasped.

'The bridge, Guns. Captain wants me.'

'Tell him the fires are out of control by the H.A. magazine. The hoists are ablaze. Ask permission to flood the magazine. Hurry! Permission to flood, d'ye hear?'

Bill heard the anxiety in the Gunner's voice. If Bill Banham wanted to flood, the situation *must* be desperate. The man's face was grey and streaked with grime.

'Right!' Tanner shouted. 'I'll be straight back.'

Then Bill found himself on the flight deck. He could barely see for the brown smoke curling along the deck; he could hardly hear for the screaming of diving Stukas. Up ahead somewhere, a pom-pom still banged away; the for'd 4.5s still barked. *The deck's hot underfoot…*

Bill started hopping from one foot to the other, his feet burning from the heat of the steel plates. He looked down and saw that the flight deck had begun to distort. He started running again, but had to throw himself flat, burning his hands, as another flight of Stukas shuddered overhead. The stern of the ship lifted into the air as she was hit again, this time on the after lift well he'd just left.

*'Dear God,'* he prayed as he scrambled to his feet. *'Save this ship.'*

He found the island then and clambered upwards. He was panting when he reached the bridge. The Captain was on the telephone:

'Tiller flat,' he snapped. 'Rudder's jammed hard-a-starboard. Right, Chief. See what you can do.' He was handing the phone to the Mid. of the Watch when he saw Bill Tanner. 'Well, what's up with the after 4.5s?' he demanded.

'Knocked out, sir. The ammunition hoists are on fire. The Gunner requests permission to flood the H.A. magazine, sir.'

Bill saw despair momentarily cross the Captain's grey face. Boyd hesitated, then spoke his thoughts aloud. 'If I flood, we've no guns. If I don't flood, we blow up.' Suddenly he turned to Tanner. 'Put the blasted fire out — but not by flooding!' he snapped. 'Go and tell 'em that.' He jammed his pipe between his teeth and turned to meet the next attack.

*What if the magazine should go up?* Bill thought. He pushed the thought away.

Anger, and a bitter hate, filled him, against the evil that did this to his ship. He glanced at his watch: three o'clock. This misery ought to be easing up soon. Where the hell was the fleet? Conspicuous by its absence, as he glanced around the horizon. At least they'd left a destroyer to pick up the pieces.

*How long will the Chief be?* he wondered. *Better remain at twenty knots until they freed the rudder, even though I'm steaming round in ever-decreasing circles. Hell, here they come again…*

He scrambled back to the bridge. Now he couldn't see them until the last moment, because of the ship's heavy list and the smoke from the fires. The Stukas screamed overhead, shuddering as they pulled out, and roared off, out of range of the guns which — though completely blind — were still firing defiantly.

The Engine Room telephone howled: 'Rudder's free, sir.' Tosswill's voice reassured his exhausted Captain. Then the Navigator and the Captain took turns to nurse the crippled carrier on to a course for Malta. It took an hour to master the technique.

'Stop the centre propeller, Pilot. Its swirl is shoving the freed rudder hard over. Hopeless like that.'

Then, quite suddenly, the last of the Stukas had disappeared. Boyd held his breath, listening for the terror of the plunging planes. Had they really gone?

'Now, let's get the old girl home.'

So, three hours and six hundred and fifty engine-orders later, Captain Denis Boyd and his Navigating Officer brought their ship under the battlements of Valletta by means of the two outer propellers only. Then, as she lined up outside the boom, the starboard lookout yelled once again:

'Alarm starboard! Green one-two-o! Torpedo bombers, sir.'

Boyd spotted them at once. 'Full ahead port,' he ordered calmly. 'Stop starboard. Open fire!'

It had been difficult enough, in all conscience, bringing the stricken carrier up the swept channel through the minefield off Filfla. Now, less than a mile from the breakwater, to have to fight off another attack, without a rudder… How, in God's name, could he comb the tracks now?

The first wave came in on the starboard bow. Charles Evans's Fulmars had landed at Hal Far after the first three attacks. Now — at this last moment, out of control, with half the guns knocked out — *Illustrious* was alone in her final ordeal.

The torpedo bombers approached in waves of three, jinking and losing height, but, strangely, they did not press home their attacks. Wops, probably… and then, after them, he heard them… *Stukas.*

Boyd's heart came into his mouth. Once more, somewhere behind him, he heard the terrifying scream of the diving Ju 87s.

'Stop port,' he cried down the voicepipe. 'Full ahead starboard.'

Check the swing… just right… NOW!

'Stop starboard.'

She'd drift through these tracks; bows steady, the slight breeze checking her. *Ah!* There they went: one whistling down the port side, two down the starboard. Bubbling and hissing, like long white eels.

*Christopher!* There were more tracks passing across his bows. Where had they come from? As he turned to search for his unseen attackers, he heard the rush of air close to him. There was a blue flash, a sudden shock wave, then the juddering of a Stuka pulling out only feet above him.

Suddenly it was very quiet. The starboard pom-poms had ceased firing. Black smoke wreathed over the bridge and he could not see.

Boyd could hear 4.5s banging away now, and from the island a staccato barking from the Royal Malta Artillery. Two more 1,000-pounders exploded somewhere close in the water. The ship jumped, and then he could see again as she emerged through the splashes. Spray from the near misses drenched them on the bridge.

'Stop both engines.'

The ship had steamed full circle and was now facing Valletta again. *Illustrious* was still afloat. Now to get her in without a rudder, without tugs…

'Look, sir!'

Richard Tosswill was pointing over the port side. An ancient dockyard tug had appeared from somewhere. Its skipper was yelling up at the towering carrier.

'British dockyard mateys are manning her, sir,' said Tosswill.

*Plucky so-and-sos*, Boyd thought. 'Ask her to take a head rope, please.'

So, almost out of control, the battered carrier entered Valletta harbour. With a rusty and fender-festooned tug threshing proudly at her bows, the great ship swung majestically past the battlements. Along the walls, by the foreshore and atop the breakwaters stood groups of Maltese. In complete silence, *Illustrious* slid by, her gaping wounds ghastly for all to see. The gun crews still stood at their posts, shells cradled in their arms, eyes turned upwards.

On the bridge an exhausted man crouched low over the voicepipe. He heard a child's voice ringing clearly across the water. The cry was taken up and, like quicksilver, the cheers echoed and re-echoed across Grand Harbour.

'Slip the tug.'

Parlatoria Wharf was less than half a cable now. *Mustn't squash the tug… no more accidents at this juncture… twenty yards… I'm drifting a bit fast… can't do anything about it now. The way's off the ship… the wharf's coming in at us awfully fast…*

*Thump!*

'Secure the ship, please, Richard.'

Denis Boyd, Captain of *Illustrious*, saw his Navigating Officer saluting him. The rest of his bridge team stood silently at attention. The Captain saluted, then hurriedly descended from the compass platform, which he had not left for five days. He hadn't eaten for thirteen hours, nor sat down for sixteen. In what remained of twilight, he must inspect his ship.

*I must see my ship, my poor, beautiful ship. Oh, God, what have they done to her? What have they done to my men?*

# CHAPTER 12

*Near Breaking Point*

The Seaman Gunner was patiently waiting his turn in the queue outside *Illustrious*'s improvised sick bay. His left arm hung numbly from its socket. He couldn't feel the pain now, but he felt uneasy about the injury: his shirt sleeve was sticky.

A mate had rolled his 'ticklers', as they called roll-your-own cigarettes, for him. He'd been on S3 pom-pom when the last bomb had struck. They'd picked him up, shaken but alive, and lugged him down here.

'Next!'

He moved inside the bulkhead. The dead and dying lay in rows along the flat. The groans from the unconscious could not be hushed, and the sick bay stank with the smell of burnt flesh, of blood and anaesthetics. There were only three men in front of him now, all worse than he. The Seaman Gunner looked away, sickened. *Think of summat else, mate. You'll wait your turn a long time yet. Drop a line to Kit…*

Like those ahead, he slithered down on his haunches, stretched his legs out ahead of him and leant against the bulkhead. With his undamaged hand he extracted the stub of a pencil from his overalls. Finally he found his threepenny notebook; holding it between his teeth he tried to rip out a leaf.

'C'mon, mate. Let me 'elp.' The man was an Ordinary Cook. *(Can't recognise you, you poor beggar. What a shocking mess your face is; lucky you can't see yourself.)*

'Thanks, Cookie.'

The Seaman Gunner moistened the point of his pencil and wrote:

*Darling Kit,*

*I hope this finds you as it leaves me in good health. The censor won't let me tell you where we are, but we are quite safe though we've had a bit of a rough time lately with a convoy.*

*This is a good ship with a good Captain. Today we were in a proper pot-mess, fires everywhere and a heavy list. I thought we were a goner. I was in S3 pom-pom. We were expecting the order to Abandon Ship, when all of a sudden the Captain came out on the wing of the bridge, smoking a pipe, as cool as a cucumber. We knew it was all right then…*

He closed his eyes. *Gawd, Kitty, I love you, lass.* For a second the image of her trim figure flashed across his imagination. Then he heard scuffling behind him and felt the cook struggling to his feet.

'Sit down, all of you,' a hoarse voice ordered gently. 'I've come to see how you are.'

The seaman felt tears springing to his eyes. Impulsively he held out his good hand.

'Thank you, sir,' he said gruffly. 'For bringing the old ship in.'

Captain Boyd nodded. His grim face was grey, drained of colour. He pressed the man's hand.

'Thank you,' he said quietly, then passed on. 'How much more have we got to take?' he whispered to himself as he strode through the sick bay. 'Haven't they dished us out enough already?'

But in fact the Luftwaffe had barely begun. Two more raids plastered Parlatoria Wharf, where the carrier lay wounded. The bomb splashes enveloped *Illustrious,* yet when the spray and smoke subsided, there she lay — still afloat, her guns still barking defiantly.

Her ship's company slept ashore in the Victoria Club, but the Captain and a nucleus stuck out the first terrible night on board, though they found little sleep in that ghastly charnel house.

Dawn broke clear on the second day. The bombers came over, hundreds of them, in a blue sky. Down they came, peeling off in their scores, straight for their stricken foe. The volunteer crews of officers in *Illustrious* struck back; they manned the remaining pom-poms, they fired the existing 4.5s until the barrels glowed red hot. The Royal Malta Artillery retaliated. Yet still the enemy came.

In a lull between raids, Captain Boyd went ashore. When he reached the dockyard wall, he looked back at his beloved ship. Her ensign still fluttered proudly in the wind, her men still fought. He squared off his cap, lit a pipe and strode towards the gate. On the crest of the ridge in the next bay lay Bighi, the naval hospital.

He forced his legs forward. He had prayed for strength to endure this worst duty of all. To suffer with the men who would see no more — to share their fears, their hopelessness, now that they could neither walk nor lead again a normal life. A day had elapsed: would they blame him a little?

The P.M.O. met him at the entrance to the ward. Denis Boyd removed his cap, raising a craggy eyebrow.

'No, sir. No more dead.'

'Thank God.'

'Lieutenant Going, sir.'

Boyd sat by Grubby's bed. The young observer was grey with pain, but the corner of his mouth twitched into a grin.

'You all right, sir? They seem to be keeping you pretty busy down there,' he said quietly. 'I can hear the old ship's guns.'

'Fine, Grubby,' the Captain said. 'Our endurance test's nearly over.'

The observer closed his eyes.

The Captain moved on. He felt that the lines of wounded would never end. But at last he had comforted the final casualty and found himself outside again, the white walls of the hospital behind him. He stood for a while to compose himself. From here, through the blinding tears, he could see the battlements of Valletta. There they stood, scarred and battered, towering over the turquoise of Grand Harbour.

Somehow, in spite of the agony of the next few days, Denis Boyd's spirit never despaired again. Day after day the enemy came. For hour after hour the ordeal continued: *Illustrious*'s endurance test and the beginning of Malta's blitz. Captain Boyd was constantly astounded by the courage and stoical stubbornness of his Maltese comrades. His ship was bringing down this wrath upon the islanders, yet they still helped all they could, did everything possible to patch up *Illustrious* so that she could sail for Alexandria. The repair work went on in between the raids.

Then, on the seventh day, the second bomb hit. It went through the pom-pom platform where the gallant Sellman and his crew were standing. It missed them by inches and exploded beneath the ship. *Illustrious* leapt from the shock.

Later, in a quiet interval, Captain Boyd sent a diver down to investigate — not a pleasant task. A bomb exploding in the water might well kill the man. He surfaced surprisingly quickly to make his report. A sizeable but unimportant hole had been blown in her bottom. Yet Captain Boyd was unhappy; so much oil had been discharged that he feared some more vital damage — but if that was the diver's report, he could not doubt it…

So the seventh day wore on. The slaughter of the enemy continued: the 87s and 88s spiralled out of the sky, to crash in black clouds amongst the rubble they had created. But still they came, the sky black with their hordes.

Bill Tanner had grown used to being a supply number on the for'd 4.5 mounting. His eyes smarted from the cordite, but he grinned in admiration at Henry Lloyd, the padre, who was strolling up and down the flight deck. He was munching a sandwich, and even from here Bill could see the man's lips moving as he chi-akked the cleaning-up parties under Commander Tuck and Rosy Baker's directions.

'Alarm red six-o!'

*Here we go again…* Bill held on tightly as the mounting spun round in its cupola. The right-hand gun started pounding away, and then Bill's left-hand gun joined in. They were yammering away: *Load, fire, stand clear of the recoil! Load, fire, stand clear…* but now the shells were exploding as they left the barrels, the rifling was so worn. It was disconcerting and dangerous.

The loading was continuing with methodical precision. Ackworth, the Gunnery Officer, was training the mounting himself, calmly issuing orders as if he was on a practice shoot.

'Local control! Rapid fire!'

Bill's heart lifted as he heard the order. The weariness slid from him as he lunged at the loading tray, rammed with his gauntleted fist. The rate of fire was up to him now.

Suddenly things went wrong. He felt the mounting swinging rapidly, so fast that he was forced to hang on to the rail. But he kept on loading and ramming, slamming the shells home, the yellow fumes of the cordite swirling, choking and blinding them in their cupola.

'Check, check, check!' Ackworth was yelling, his face white. He'd raised his hands from the firing lever, but was still peering along the sights. 'The training's run wild — cease firing!'

The right-hand gun was still blazing away, so Bill leapt across and tapped the loader, another pilot, on the shoulder. Above the scream of diving Stukas, they heard Ackworth yelling:

'Bill, nip up and see if the chaps on the bridge are all right. We were firing directly at them.'

His heart hammering, Bill ignored the pandemonium in the sky above. Still wearing his asbestos gauntlets, he ran for the bridge. The control personnel, the Captain amongst them, were picking themselves up and cautiously peeping over the for'd lip of the bridge.

'Gunnery Officer's apologies, sir,' Bill said nervously, 'but are you all right? The mounting ran wild, sir.'

There was a moment's silence, then Captain Boyd turned round, his eyes smouldering.

'Tell him, Sub-Lieutenant Tanner, that he nearly achieved what the Luftwaffe has been endeavouring to do for eight days.' He turned to his Navigating Officer. 'I'm going ashore, Richard.' He grinned. 'It's safer there. I want to see what the bomb did to the Junior Officers' Club.'

Bill stood aside. The Captain winked. 'Give Guns a kick in the pants from me,' he said.

Captain Boyd emerged from the smoking ruins of the J.O.C. and stood gazing up at his ship. Another three days and the dockyard would have her patched up sufficiently to put to sea for Alexandria.

Looking out across the harbour he sighted the leader of the Fourteenth Destroyer Flotilla nosing round the breakwater. Here was his escort. Good old *Jervis!* It was Philip Mack, the

Captain 'D', come with two others of his veterans to see them safely through. Mack was standing unconcernedly on his bridge as he manoeuvred *Jervis* in the middle of Grand Harbour. The wake boiled at her stern; around her the turquoise of the deep water seethed from the shell-splinters falling from anti-aircraft shells as they burst in the sky.

*He's coming alongside Illustrious… a dangerous berth for him. The Stukas have hit that ammunition ship, the Essex.*

Scuttling down *Illustrious*'s gangways, he could see Tuck and Rosy Baker dragging fire hoses after them along the quay. Their fire parties would have to get a hustle on if they were to prevent 4,000 tons of ammunition going up.

Captain Boyd hurried back to *Illustrious.* He reached the port after sponson as his old friend swung alongside. The head rope was hauled across, and then he saw Philip below him, saluting as he looked up. His presence exuded confidence.

'Hullo, Philip,' *Illustrious*'s Captain called down. 'This isn't a particularly healthy berth, you know.'

Captain D.14, a broad, powerful man, was grinning up at him.

'If you can take it, so can we,' Mack replied.

Boyd nodded, his heart lifting. This was typical of Mack. *Illustrious* was no longer alone.

# CHAPTER 13

## *The Approach*

When *Illustrious* had been patched up sufficiently in Alexandria, she sailed round the Cape to the United States for repair. Her aircraft were dispersed to carry on annoying the enemy. Her former Captain, now Rear Admiral Boyd, had hoisted his flag in *Formidable*, who had arrived in Port Said on the 9th of March. He had transferred as many of his officers and men as he could, and was hoping to gather his dispersed fliers around him again. Of these, Bill Tanner and five others of 815 Squadron — under its new leader, Torrens-Spence — were operating their Swordfish from Maleme airfield in Crete. The new carrier, of similar design to *Illustrious* and with an armoured deck, began urgently to train her squadrons. By the 25th of March 1941, she was fully operational.

On the afternoon of the 27th the Japanese Consul, who was a conscientious member of the golf club, was sitting idly outside the club room waiting for his partner. Of massive proportions despite his diminutive height, he was known amongst the Commander-in-Chief's staff as 'The Blunt End of the Axis'. He was also known as a reporter of every fleet movement to his Nazi accomplices.

Lifting his heavy lids, he peered at the Britishers walking across the grass. Ah, yes — the Commander-in-Chief with one of his staff. They were laughing, and Admiral Cunningham was carrying his night suitcase.

'Sorry to keep you waiting, Consul.' The Japanese diplomat looked up at his partner, the Egyptian attaché from the Embassy, who was a slightly built, suave man with a deeply lined face.

'No matter,' the Consul purred. 'There's no hurry. We will follow the Admiral round.'

The Consul and his friend enjoyed their round. They enjoyed, too, their drinks afterwards. The Consul lingered longer than usual that night; after watching the Admiral leave at dusk, there was no pressing necessity for him to return to his Consulate. In fact, he enjoyed the evening. The shore staff of the Royal Navy were at last becoming more friendly.

He slept soundly that night, and awoke later than usual on the 28th of March 1941. Clambering from his bed he clumped across to the window overlooking the magnificent harbour and flung open the shutters. His eyes swept across the wide expanse of water. The harbour was empty.

At 0740 on the morning of the 28th of March, Force B was sixty miles south of the island of Gavdos, off the southern coast of Crete. This Force was commanded by Vice-Admiral Pridham-Wippell (V.A. Light Forces) who was flying his flag in the 6-inch cruiser *Orion.* In company were the Royal Australian Navy's cruiser *Perth;* screening them were the destroyers *Ilex* (Captain D.2), *Hasty, Hereward* and *Vendetta.* This force had earlier sighted an enemy reconnaissance aircraft — not an unusual occurrence except that the plane was an Ro.43, an aircraft carried by Italian cruisers. The enemy *must* be at sea.

Five minutes earlier, the Vice-Admiral had intercepted two enemy reports from the dawn search which had been flown off by *Formidable;* the aircraft carrier was with Force A, 150 miles to the south-eastwards and steering north-westwards at twenty knots. Aircraft 5B and 5F had reported two separate enemy cruiser forces within thirty miles of V.A.L.F's own position. Because of the reputed inaccuracy of aircraft reporting, it was assumed that V.A.L.F's own ships, Force B, had been reported by *Formidable*'s aircraft. Vice-Admiral Pridham-Wippell was still puzzling out the significance of the sighting of the Ro.43 when a lookout shouted from the port wing:

'Smoke bearing red one-seven-o, sir!'

Ten minutes later V.A.L.F. had worked up to full speed, but was worried by having identified the ships that were overhauling him as three Zam-class cruisers and three Ascari destroyers. These were 8-inch gun cruisers and were two-and-a-half knots faster than his own 6-inch cruisers. The enemy could therefore overhaul Force B, stand off while they outgunned their British targets, then pick off each British cruiser at will. V.A.L.F. therefore decided to lead his pursuers towards the Commander-in-Chief who, with his battleships, was closing up from the south-eastwards.

At 0812 the enemy cruisers opened fire. Their shooting from thirteen miles was accurate: the enemy seemed to be concentrating upon *Gloucester*, who was straddled continuously. Disappearing behind the leaping columns of spurting water, she 'snaked' the line to throw off the Italian gunlayers.

By 0829 the enemy had overhauled Force B, so that *Gloucester*, with her modern 6-inch guns, thought she could engage at extreme range. A minute after opening fire, she catapulted her Walrus amphibian aircraft for spotting duties.

*Gloucester* ceased fire after three salvoes because they had fallen short. The enemy, however, altered course to draw outside British gun-range. Then, at 0838, they altered course parallel to the British cruisers and resumed firing.

It was at this moment that the Vice-Admiral in *Orion* became worried. One of the screen, *Vendetta* — an old warrior 'V & W' destroyer from the First War — was developing engine trouble and falling astern. V.A.L.F. told her to draw out to starboard and to return independently to Alexandria. At that moment also, aircraft 5F's enemy report came through: *3 battleships to the north-west of Force B.*

Vice-Admiral Pridham-Wippell realised that this was probably a wrong identification by aircraft 5F reporting the British cruisers in error. At 0855 the enemy cruisers turned away to port and disappeared to the north-westward at twenty-eight knots. The British force turned also to shadow and report. At 0936 V.A.L.F. reported to his C.-in-C., now only thirty miles distant, that the enemy's cruisers were steering 3200 at twenty-eight knots and were sixteen miles away.

V.A.L.F. continued the chase. The enemy cruisers were hull-down when there was a yell from *Orion*'s director tower:

'Large ship bearing red eight-o!'

The Vice-Admiral swung his binoculars to the bearing. It was an enemy battleship all right, and a Veneto at that. V.A.L.F. felt uncomfortably placed. The jaws of the trap into which Force B had steamed were about to snap. He would have been even more worried if he'd known that another Italian cruiser force was bearing down on him from the north-east. *Gloucester*'s Walrus had at 0917 sighted five more enemy cruisers steering west. But this report never reached *Orion.*

Nothing could save the British cruisers now: the trap had sprung.

The pride of the Italian fleet was their two new battleships the *Vittorio Veneto* and the *Littorio.* The Italian Commander-in-Chief, Admiral Iachino, was flying his flag in the *Vittorio Veneto* on the morning of the 28th of March: the *Littorio* had been hit twice by torpedo bombers at Taranto.

Admiral Iachino, though proud of his fleet and of himself, was not brimming over with enthusiasm: the Regia Aeronautica and the Luftwaffe — in spite of their promises — were letting him down. So far, apart from a dawn enemy report from the Ro.43, he had little information on which to deploy his forces. Uncertain of himself, he peered through the armoured slit of his bridge in the *Vittorio Veneto.*

It was a wise decision, he thought, to turn back his Force Z. They were too far east and, if the British aircraft carrier *was* at sea, her aircraft would soon attack his cruiser force. Vice-Admiral Cattaneo in the *Zara* was a fine man, but at times he needed restraining.

Iachino smiled as he looked at his watch: 1055. The great battleship was scything like a destroyer through this calm sea. At thirty knots her own screen of four destroyers was hard put to keep up. They'd soon be sighting the British cruisers that were so rashly chasing his Force X: Vice-Admiral Sansonetti in *Trieste,* and the *Trento* and *Bolzano,* with their three screening destroyers.

The *Veneto,* with her giant 305-millimetre guns already trained on the expected bearing, would be able to pick off the British cruisers, one by one, in this visibility of over fifteen miles.

'Enemy in sight! Green four-o.'

Admiral Iachino's heart quickened.

'Permission to open fire, sir?' the Flag Captain called up the voicepipe.

'Open fire!' Iachino controlled the excitement in his voice. He lifted his binoculars to observe the fall of shot after the great guns had roared. *Now I've got 'em,* he thought. *They've run right into my trap.*

On the Admiral's bridge in *Warspite,* the Commander-in-Chief cheerfully paid up a ten-shilling bet he'd lost with Commander Power. V.A.L.F.'s cruisers had been in action with a group of 8-inch enemy cruisers to the north-westward. It looked as if the Italians had come out to fight after all. The bait had worked.

The bridge clock showed 0833.

'Tell *Formidable* to range her torpedo strike,' Admiral Cunningham snapped, pacing up and down the Admiral's bridge like a caged tiger. 'The pressure on Pridham-Wippell needs relieving.'

*Warspite* ordered *Valiant* to forge on ahead in support of V.A.L.F. Admiral Cunningham watched jealously as the great battleship began to gain bearing on *Warspite*'s port quarter. It was the same old story: chasing a faster enemy.

The bad luck was beyond bearing this morning. Firstly, the fleet had to wait for *Formidable* every time she turned out of the line to fly off her aircraft: what little breeze there was, was easterly. Secondly, *Warspite*'s speed was restricted to 20 knots: she had 'condenseritis' after passing too close to a mud bank on leaving Alex.

A.B.C. watched angrily as *Valiant* forged ahead at full speed, her bow wave white in the morning sun. He knew that *Warspite*'s Commander (E) was sick in Alex, but then he remembered that Captain Wilkinson, the Fleet Engineer Officer, was on board.

'Do something about our speed,' Admiral Cunningham ordered. Captain Wilkinson disappeared below into *Warspite*'s engine room. 'Tell the Fleet Air Arm at Maleme to attack the enemy cruisers with torpedoes,' the Admiral continued. 'Quote the enemy's position.'

'Aye, aye, sir.' It was 0849.

Admiral Cunningham glared across at *Valiant,* but she was gaining no more. *Warspite* must be increasing speed again. *Thank God! Now we can all go on together.*

But the C.-in-C. was worried. V.A.L.F. was in trouble, yet where was the enemy battle fleet? Once he had committed *Formidable*'s striking force, it would be at least two hours before she was able to mount another.

'Enemy cruisers have broken off action with Force B, sir,' Commander Power reported. 'They're steering north-west, and V.A.L.F. is shadowing, sir.'

'Very good.' *Better wait until the situation clarifies,* Admiral Cunningham thought. *I'll hold back the torpedo bombers and ask the R.A.F. 201 Group to shadow the enemy.* The presence of a carrier-borne aircraft would indicate that the Med fleet was at sea.

The chase continued, V.A.L.F. shadowing and reporting the enemy cruisers steaming north-westerly ahead of Force B. *If only I could slow them down,* Admiral Cunningham thought. Suddenly he made up his mind.

'Send the following to Formidable,' C.-in-C. snapped as he prowled in his cage. 'Fly off torpedo strike to attack cruisers in sight of V.A.L.F., or other squadrons of cruisers if sighted.'

The time was 0936. At this and every other moment of the day, there was only one predominant thought in the Commander-in-Chief's mind: to bring the enemy battle fleet within gun range.

# CHAPTER 14

*Torpedo Bombers*

'Damn shame about old *York,* Brandy,' Bill Tanner remarked to his observer, as they strolled out on to the freshly constructed Maleme airfield on the island of Crete. With their bare hands they had helped to turn these barren fields into a flat enough plateau for their Swordfish. 'I did my Snotty's time in her in the West Indies.'

Brandy nodded. 'Those explosive boats had guts though, Bill. The survivors said the charges were fixed in the bows.'

'The old ship looks so forlorn beached there in Souda Bay, Brandy,' Bill went on. 'Her engine and boiler rooms are flooded.'

'The worst setback is that now we're only in contact with C.-in-C. through our shaky W/T pack,' the observer continued. '*York*'s W/T office is out of action.'

'The pack did us all right for our dawn patrol, Brandy. You were in touch, weren't you?'

'Just.' Brandy kicked the yellow earth. 'Bill, I do miss old *Illustrious.*'

'Same here, chum.'

They were silent for a moment as they looked across at the four Stringbags that had just landed. A group of mechanics swarmed over L5T, which had experienced engine trouble.

'I miss a carrier,' Brandy continued dreamily. 'I miss Denis Boyd and the boys.' Suddenly he chuckled. 'Wonder what the "Old Man" is like, now he's an Admiral?'

'815's just as good, Brandy,' Bill tried to console his young observer. 'George Beale is as good a C.O. as the others.'

'Sure, Bill, but this dump's just not the same.' He looked up. 'My God,' he whispered. 'Look who's here!'

Bill groaned as he watched the slight figure picking its way carefully across the pebbles. He could recognise that pedantic stride anywhere.

'What the hell's *he* doing here?' he muttered. 'Thought we'd left him behind in Alex.'

Brandy saluted and Bill reluctantly followed suit.

'Good morning, Tanner,' Kyne said brightly. 'Seen the C.O.?'

'No, sir. We've only just landed from our dawn patrol.'

'Busy, are you?' Kyne looked round, his sandy eyebrows raised. 'Refuelling already?'

'Things are pretty hectic here, sir.'

'Bit much for you, eh?' Kyne flicked a pebble between his thumb and forefinger. 'As a matter of fact I've come up from Souda especially about you, Tanner.'

'Yes…?' Bill felt Brandy moving out of earshot.

'An M.T.B. is giving me a passage to Malta to fix up a court-martial. She's put in to Souda to refuel and to drop off some C.B.s.' Kyne rubbed his chin. 'I thought I'd take advantage of the two hours to come up to see you and the C.O.'

Bill looked the Lieutenant-Commander full in the face, but Kyne's pale eyes wandered away towards the Swordfish.

'Why d'you want to see me, sir?' Bill felt his heart hammering. It couldn't be… surely his case was closed?

'It's *your* court-martial, Tanner.' Kyne smiled for a moment, then laid his hand on the young pilot's sleeve. 'The Provost Marshal has recommended that your case be tried on Malta as there are no facilities here in Crete.'

Bill hesitated, wrestling with his self-control. Dammit, they were fighting a war here…

'I thought the inquiry settled all that, sir?' he blurted.

'No, Tanner. They decided there was a *prima facie* case. Discipline has got to be maintained out here. There's too much laxity.'

Kyne turned on his heel. Bill stood motionless, his fists clenched.

'All pilots report to the briefing hut!'

Pilot and observer glanced at each other, then broke into a run as they raced for the dilapidated hovel that controlled all operations. George Beale, the C.O., was waiting for them.

'Look carefully, chums. I've sketched this out from the info we've received from the enemy reports.'

'Are the Eyeties out, sir?' Brandy asked.

'Reckon so: *Formidable* has flown off a strike. We've been ordered to do the same, but we've only just received the signal.'

They crouched over the plan that the C.O. had traced in the sand.

'Our orders are to attack this force of enemy cruisers: three *Trento* 8-inch cruisers with an escort of three destroyers. Excuse me —' Beale pushed past Lieutenant-Commander Kyne — 'I'm afraid I can't see you now. We're just off.' The C.O. squatted on his haunches. 'Tanner, you be tail-end Charlie, will you? We haven't got a spare fish for you, but you'll be useful.'

'I can report and observe, sir,' Bill grinned. 'Better than nothing. I'll bring the air gunner and we can cover.'

'Depth setting, 20 feet. Safety range, 400 yards. Torpedo speed, 40 knots. Any questions? I want to get going, so make it snappy. Force B's in trouble.'

'Return to Maleme, sir?'

'Yes. Get cracking!'

They nearly knocked over Kyne in the scramble. 'Sorry we can't stop, sir,' Bill shouted over his shoulder. 'See you in Malta!'

The Swordfish had already started up. Beneath the bellies of the other three gleamed the only Mark XII torpedoes left on the island. By 1050 the last of the four Swordfish had rumbled down the scorched runway and taken off. They climbed to 9,000 feet, the three torpedo bombers in one Vic, with Bill wheeling above them. Taking a departure from Elaphonisi, they flew due south, at 1130 leaving Gavdos Island twenty miles to port, a mauve haze in the middle of the Mediterranean. Twenty-five minutes later, Geoffrey Martin's wingtips rocked.

There, nine thousand feet below them, like toy boats on the turquoise surface of a swimming pool, three large ships were steaming in line ahead. Ahead of them, in line abreast, three destroyers formed a protective anti-submarine screen. Bill chuckled. At the speed they were doing (at least twenty-eight knots, judging by their wakes, and by their bow waves fanning out abreast their forward funnels) the destroyers would be ineffective against the British submarines. Strung out ahead like this, they were leaving the flanks wide open for the Swordfish. If Geoffrey Martin could take his Vic over to the enemy's port side, they'd be attacking 'up-sun' — the perfect attacking position.

Bill waited, his eyes skinned for enemy fighters. He blew down the Gosport to the air gunner: 'Keep a good look out.'

'Aye, aye, sir.' It was good to hear Birley's confident voice. The gunner was a taciturn type and good with the Vickers.

The cruisers were beneath them now, but three miles on their starboard beam. With their twin funnels they looked like Cavours, but they weren't large enough for battleships. At that instant Brander called up from the observer's cockpit:

'Reckon they're Trentos.'

'Whack out an enemy report, then,' Bill shouted. 'Three 8-in cruisers, course 300 degrees, speed thirty knots, from our position.'

'Right! Look — there they go...!'

The three Swordfish had formed in line ahead; they were staggered for height, one stepped up above the other.

Bill watched the nose of the first Stringbag suddenly tilt downwards. Down they swooped, down, down...

The height wound rapidly off the altimeter as Bill tried to follow them. *Strange that there's no flak yet,* he thought. Three thousand, two, one thousand... the ships were much larger now, fine on the starboard bows of the Swordfish now that the torpedo bombers had turned parallel to the cruisers' course. Seven hundred, six...

*Better stay here,* Bill decided; *I can't help much more. Oh God, wish I had a kipper...*

He eased back on the stick; the howl in the rigging diminished. The torpedo strike was down to deck level now. Jinking and weaving in line ahead, they had gained enough bearing for the run-in...

*There goes the C.O.!*

The leading torpedo bomber had turned suddenly to starboard. At that instant every gun from the cruiser squadron opened fire. The sky was thick with brown cordite fumes, the air black around the Stringbags. Then came the tracer, visible even in this bright daylight, and floating slowly towards the attacking aircraft.

Bill held his breath. God, how slow the lumbering Stringbags seemed! The second aircraft had held on before turning, and tail-end Charlie had gone even farther. Now they were all diving into the attack…

Geoffrey Martin had taken the after cruiser, Kiggell the middle one, while the last Swordfish was hell-bent on the leader. Dammit, the cruisers were already altering course, their slender hulls listing heavily as they wheeled. The sun was shining upon their grey upperworks, and their wakes sparkled and leapt in threshing foam.

The C.O. had dropped his torpedo. His aircraft was lifting now. There went the fish — *splash!* — as it hit the water, thirty feet below the fuselage of the aircraft.

'Look!' Bill shouted over the tube. 'The C.O.'s dropped.'

'Right!' Brandy yelled. 'I'm making a sketch map.'

The after cruiser had turned away now, her stern combing the C.O.'s torpedo track. Kiggell must have also dropped: his crate was standing on its end as it soared upwards. *Must have dropped at about three thousand yards… Hullo, what's happened to the rear Swordfish? She's held on — too high. Ah, there she goes, right through the flak. She's attacking the centre cruiser which is turning towards… might catch her on the bow as she swings — there goes the fish!*

Bill hovered a few seconds longer to observe the three torpedo tracks. The first two passed astern of the rear ship, while the last one slid down the port side of the centre cruiser.

Bill felt like weeping. *All torpedoes missed… no hits… better report it.*

'Brandy?' he shouted down the tube. 'Tell C.-in-C., *No hits.*'

'Hey, look out!' It was Brandy on the Gosport. A barrage of flak was bursting ahead of them. Bill hauled back the stick; the engine roared as he gave her all he had. Then, at 800 feet, the aircraft juddered from a sudden shock.

'Bill! Petrol's pouring out of the line!' It was Brandy; he sounded worried. 'We're hit. Must have been about their last salvo, too…'

'I'll gain height. What's my course for the fleet, Brandy?' Bill kept climbing… 1,200, 1,500…

'070 degrees,' Brandy yelled. 'If we really have to ditch, we should be in the line of advance of our cruisers or battle fleet.'

'O.K.,' Bill shouted. 'Prepare to abandon aircraft.' He glanced at the fuel gauge — already the pointer had fallen away.

*God! What a way to finish the war…*

Later that morning three Albacores and two Swordfish of 829 Squadron were circuiting above *Formidable.* Higher still, the two Fulmar fighters of 803 Squadron wheeled and twisted. An earlier sortie by Saunt's 826 Squadron had caused *Veneto* to break off her attack on Force B's cruisers.

Admiral Boyd turned to watch the flying-off of the last aircraft. 'Where's this Walrus come from?' he asked.

'Looks like *Gloucester*'s spotter, sir. She's requested to land on. She's picked up the crew of a ditched Swordfish from Maleme.'

'Hurry up, then. I want to rejoin C.-in-C.'

Rear Admiral (Air) watched the unwieldy amphibian lumbering down the flight deck. Three wet figures were lying along the main plane.

At 1244, *Formidable* swung away from the easterly wind and worked up to full speed to rejoin the battle fleet, which had now dipped below the western horizon. The opportunity was snatched for a hurried meal, and food was taken round to the gun crews who could not leave their mountings.

The Admiral was chewing his corned-beef sandwiches when he saw before him two scruffy aircrew in borrowed clothes.

'Where the devil have you come from, Tanner?'

'Picked out of the drink, sir, by *Gloucester*'s Walrus. We were in the Maleme strike, sir.'

The Admiral continued chewing. 'Well, what d'you want, eh?' he grunted.

'Request permission to fly off in the spare Walrus, sir. We could help with shadowing.'

The Admiral hesitated. This was the lad under a cloud — Bill Tanner, the Sub-Lieutenant due for court-martial in Malta.

'Does the Captain agree, Tanner?'

'Yes, sir, if you approve.'

'All right, then, but I can't wait for you,' he grunted. 'Follow *Gloucester*'s Walrus when she takes off.'

'Aye, aye, sir. She's refuelling now. Thank you, sir.'

The two young men saluted like erring schoolboys. Boyd smiled to himself. Then he heard the Captain calling:

'Alarm starboard! Green two-five, enemy aircraft!'

The Admiral (Air) leapt for the side of the bridge. Dammit, how had this S79 torpedo bomber penetrated their fighter screen? Look at it, just above the sea and less than two thousand yards off. Why were the guns silent?

He heard the Captain bellowing over the bridge. 1,000 yards now and still coming in. *Splash!* — there went her torpedo…

The pom-poms suddenly shook off their spell and rumbled into action.

'Hard-a-starboard!' the Admiral heard the Captain shouting. *Formidable* listed as she swung to her rudder. Slowly, so painfully slowly, she began to comb the track of the advancing torpedo. *The fish must be here any second now…*

'Alarm starboard! Green two-o!'

The Captain yelled again: there was another S79, fine on the starboard bow… He had already checked the ship's swing when once again he leapt for the voicepipe. 'Hard-a-starboard!'

The first torpedo went bubbling down the port side; the Admiral saw its track, like a long white finger. *But now the other fish is bound to strike us,* he thought. *This will put us out of the fight.* Veneto *will escape now… How the devil did these torpedo bombers slink in unawares? Must be the low visibility on the surface…*

They held their breath while the seconds passed. Once again the aircraft banked through the hail of machine-gun and pom-pom fire. Then they knew they were safe; by now the torpedo must have passed.

Rear Admiral (Air) pursed his lips, blew out his cheeks and sighed. *Formidable* resumed her course, headed for the fleet, and by 1400 she was in station again. Then occurred one of those small miracles which sometimes alter the fate of the world: the breeze suddenly veered from easterly to westerly. Now *Formidable* could operate her aircraft without leaving the battle line. The battleships would not now have to wait for her. There was a chance, after all, of bringing the enemy battleships to action. If only one of *Formidable*'s Second Strike aircraft could wing her, the *Veneto*'s fate would be sealed.

Rear Admiral Boyd heard the Commander (Flying) reporting to the Captain: 'Permission to fly off the two Walrus, sir?'

'Carry on, please.'

Boyd leant over the wing of his bridge. He watched *Gloucester*'s Walrus take off, then down the flight deck rumbled the second of the two amphibians with Sub-Lieutenant Tanner at the controls. For a split second, the Admiral caught sight of the pilot, his face set in concentration as he took off. But

Tanner had given his orders to his observer. The Midshipman saluted the Admiral's bridge as they flashed by.

*Poor blighter,* thought Rear Admiral Boyd. *What's the good of Courts of Inquiry during wartime? I hope Tanner does well today, then perhaps I can quash the absurdity of his court-martial.*

'Better fly off three search Albacores,' Boyd ordered. He looked up at the second striking force, still circling overhead. He dared not lose them until the enemy's position was pinpointed. 'Tell our Walrus to go on ahead, Flag Lieutenant.'

'Aye, aye, sir.'

Boyd watched Tanner's pusher biplane draw slowly ahead. The afternoon wore on while they all waited. The great ships were steaming at full speed in open order: *Warspite,* the flagship, *Valiant, Barham,* and then *Formidable.* What majesty, what power they represented!

Overhead the second torpedo strike waited to pounce.

'Enemy report from aircraft 4F,' the Staff Officer said hurriedly, 'putting the *Veneto* sixty-five miles ahead. Her course 300 degrees, speed 30 knots.' The officer was breathless. 'From C.-in-C., sir: *Send in your second torpedo strike now.'*

Boyd nodded, then glanced at his watch. 'Tell the Second Strike to proceed in execution of previous orders, Flags. Give them the enemy battleship's position.'

The time was three minutes past three in the afternoon.

# CHAPTER 15

## *Second Strike*

Admiral Iachino, Commander-in-Chief of the Italian battle fleet, felt uneasy. He knew he should have destroyed that British cruiser squadron. To hell with those British torpedo bombers! If only they hadn't attacked at that moment... a victory had been snatched from beneath the barrels of his guns.

Since the attack of the torpedo aircraft at 1127, Iachino had concentrated his forces. Force X (the three *Trento* cruisers and their screen) was less than seven miles ahead. During this run to the north-westward at thirty knots, *Veneto* had been regularly bombed by Royal Air Force Blenheim bombers. Though the high-level attacks were accurate, no ship had so far been hit.

Admiral Iachino was obeying instructions. Though the object of the sortie of his fleet was the destruction of the British convoys to Crete and Greece, he had strict orders not to risk his battleship in action with the British fleet. With his superior speed, this was undoubtedly the correct strategy; it had been successful so far, both at Cape Spartivento and off Calabria.

Judging by the meagre reports on the enemy from shore D/F fixes and from his own reconnaissance aircraft, Iachino must assume from the appearance of carrier-borne aircraft that *Formidable* was at sea. If she was, it was probable that Admiral Cunningham was also sweeping the Mediterranean with his fleet. His adversary had not yet missed a chance.

Iachino glanced at his watch: 1518. He picked up his binoculars and slowly swept the horizon: there was his destroyer screen, a destroyer stationed at fifteen hundred metres on either bow. He continued sweeping round to port and then through the funnel haze to right astern. Nothing in sight except that shadowy Walrus, hull-down on the horizon. Blast it! If only the Luftwaffe had sent out its promised air support…

*'Guarda! Guarda!* Green four-o, formation of enemy bombers! Angle of sight seven-o, height 8,000 feet.'

The H.A. guns immediately opened fire. He could see the white cotton-wool puffs bursting amongst the Blenheims. *Santa Maria*, but it was difficult to hit an aircraft! Those R.A.F. pilots had courage: nothing broke up their formation.

*There they go!* He sighed with relief as the bombs dropped. Down they toppled, black specks growing larger at every second. Iachino controlled his instinct to duck, to cower from these terrifying bombs.

*Whee-ee! Whee-ee!* The stick fell right across his bows, smothering the bridge with spray.

*'Guarda!'* a lookout screamed from the starboard wing. He was pointing along the starboard quarter where, barely three hundred metres distant, two fighters swept in low, dipping and wheeling, their guns spitting and chattering.

Admiral Iachino nipped back into his armoured bridge. He heard the bullets splattering against the steel. 'Open fire!' he yelled. 'What are you waiting for?'

He saw the close-range crews, mesmerised by shock, sheltering from the hail of bullets. He saw the tails of the Fulmars curvetting and twisting as they passed over the for'd turrets. Then, to his amazement, he saw the destroyer on his port bow swinging to port as her guns opened fire.

What the…?

His heart missed a beat as from out of the sun dropped three torpedo bombers. They were inside the screen already, and peeling off as they separated… already two were right ahead, and were fine on his starboard bow, a thousand metres away.

'Hard-a-starboard!' he heard the Captain yelling on the bridge. 'Hard-a-starboard! Open fire! Green one-o!'

*Formidable*'s Walrus was three miles on the enemy battleship's port quarter as the second striking force swept past, five hundred yards on Bill Tanner's starboard bow. They were at 5,000 feet and Bill plainly saw Dalyell-Stead, 829's C.O., raise his hand in greeting, his sub-flight of three Albacores gaining bearing as they climbed. Because the Albacore gained height more rapidly than the Swordfish, the second sub-flight of two Swordfish — 5K and 4B — was a mile astern. By forging ahead, Dalyell-Stead was obviously trying to coordinate the attack: both sub-flights would go in together.

Bill felt the tension mounting as the seconds ticked by. The whole battle of the Mediterranean could turn on the next few minutes. A handful of brave men in five obsolescent aircraft. The *Veneto* steaming so peacefully there, her sleek outline a masterpiece of the naval architect's skill. In her light grey, she appeared to glide across the ultramarine of this ancient sea. A modern destroyer was weaving on her port bow while another screened her a mile ahead. They weren't making much wake: speed about 24 knots, course 270 degrees.

*Look, Dalyell-Stead's detaching the fighters…* Bill watched the two Fulmars streaking past the nearest destroyer, just as a stick of bombs plumped across the battleship's bows. *Good old R.A.F.! Couldn't have timed it better.*

'There they go, Brandy!' Bill nudged his observer, who, in the relatively spacious cockpit of the amphibian, had come up close to his pilot to observe and record. 'There goes Dalyell-Stead…'

Lieutenant-Commander Dalyell-Stead dropped from 5,000 feet in between the two destroyers. With himself in 5H, he flew with 5G in between the escort, while 5H swung outside the leading destroyer in order to disperse the attack. Bill watched them drop to sea level, just as the two Fulmars flashed across *Veneto* to beat up the battleship's close-range emplacements.

Bill held his breath. So far, only the leading destroyer had reacted. The battleship was still silent, except for sporadic fire at the disappearing Blenheims.

Two thousand yards… fifteen hundred… What had happened? They were right down on the sea now and steadying for their final approach… God! Dalyell-Stead was going in on the engaged side!

Bill's thoughts were shattered by the eruption of the battleship into an inferno of H.A. fire. Dalyell-Stead had gambled on approaching through the fire of the 6-inch H.A. while they were still firing at the retreating Blenheims. His incredible decision had brought him luck until now… but he couldn't survive this. Bill tried to turn his head away. How could that Albacore survive the hail of bullets?

Dalyell-Stead held steady, then Bill saw his torpedo splashing a thousand yards fine on the port bow of the battleship which had started to swing to starboard, away from the torpedo. Her close-range weapons were now opening up with all they had. Her speed on turning had dropped right away. The C.O.'s torpedo *must* hit. He couldn't miss at that suicidal range…

Bill saw 5H dip momentarily, then lift herself over the bows of the battleship, barely twenty yards ahead. As she turned desperately to port, she presented her starboard side squarely to the gunners. God, what terrible punishment those gallant men were taking…

He saw the Albacore shudder, then pick up momentarily. Suddenly it dipped, then began falling.

Bill couldn't tear his eyes away as the stricken 5H dived straight for the sea, a thousand yards on the battleship's bow. The *Veneto* was now halfway through her turn. Sickened, Bill saw Dalyell-Stead plunge into the Mediterranean. He'd never had a chance.

The splash and foam subsided as 5F and 5G pulled away to gain height. A second after Dalyell-Stead perished, a fountain of water and an orange flash appeared on the battleship's port quarter.

'A hit!' Brandy yelled. 'Bill, he's hit her!'

Bill could have wept in his excitement. Dalyell-Stead had not even the satisfaction of witnessing the success of his attack. He had died before the torpedo had struck.

'There goes the second sub-flight!' It was Brandy again, pointing through the open hatchway.

5K and 5B were running in now. As the battleship turned slowly back on to her reciprocal course, she presented the whole length of her starboard side to the second sub-flight, already down to thirty feet. There went the fish, dropped at about twelve hundred yards. The flak was thick amongst the Swordfish. Jinking and weaving, they clawed for height, turned on their tails, and ran for home.

It was all over. The battleship was stopped, great smoke rings shooting from her funnels.

Bill turned to his observer. 'Don't just sit there, boy!' he shouted. 'Tell 'em, for Pete's sake. Tell 'em the enemy's hit.'

Dalyell-Stead had given his life. He, his observer Cooke, and the Petty Officer air gunner, Blankhorn, had perished, but in one glorious moment they had halted the pride of the enemy's fleet.

Now it was up to the battleships…

From C.-in-C. to Rear Admiral (Air) *Formidable: Well done. Give her another nudge at dusk. Time of origin 1600.*

Rear Admiral Boyd smiled grimly. His fliers had stopped her once, but now, from the shadower's enemy reports, she was evidently under way again — and her speed was nineteen knots. Boyd was in despair. *Our fleet will never catch her now.* Was 5H's crew to have perished in vain?

He turned to Bissett, Captain of *Formidable.* 'I want every strike aircraft you can find. Muster every available aircraft and we'll strike again at dusk.'

Sunset was at 1840. At 1720, the C.-in-C. ordered the destroyers under Captain Mack (D.14) in *Jervis* to form up for a night torpedo attack. At 1810, Admiral Cunningham made a general signal to clarify his intentions:

*If cruisers gain touch with damaged battleship, 2nd and 14th Destroyer Flotillas will be sent to attack. If she is not then destroyed, battle fleet will follow in. If not located by cruisers, I intend to work round to the north and then west, and regain touch in the morning.*

At 1745 *Warspite*'s Walrus was catapulted to relieve the exhausted shadowers. At 1830 Lieutenant-Commander Bolt, D.S.C., an experienced observer, began transmitting a string of amplifying reports which cleared up the confusion in C.-in-C.'s mind. Bill Tanner, nearly out of fuel in his Walrus, flopped down on *Formidable*'s flight deck. On his return journey he had sighted *Formidable*'s dusk strike flying overhead at five thousand feet. Bill counted six Albacores and two Swordfish, each with a torpedo nestling between their wheels. Saunt was leading them again in 4A. For Abrams, Tuke and Williams in 4K, 4P and 5A, this too was their second strike today. They must be dead beat.

Bill smiled grimly to himself as he walked stiffly across the flight deck. 'What is there to laugh at, for Pete's sake?' Brandy asked testily.

'I'm just wondering about our Maleme chums from Squadron 815,' Bill chuckled. 'I bet Torrens-Spence will be there.'

'What's so funny?'

'Just the thought that he might be short of aircrew.'

'So what?'

'He might have been forced to press-gang Kyne.'

Lieutenant F. M. A. Torrens-Spence, R.N., was waiting impatiently for sunset. Both Kiggell and himself had sighted the enemy at 1810, twenty-five miles off. They had dropped astern of the Italian fleet and shadowed at five miles. The wait was getting on Torrens-Spence's nerves.

Sunset was 1840. Twilight would not end until 1930. He had decided to wait until then for his dusk attack, when the Italian ships would be silhouetted against the last streaks of twilight.

The C.O. of the two Maleme Swordfish admiringly watched the concentration of those fine Italian ships below him. Listing and wheeling, they were reforming into a compact mass: the battleship, *Veneto,* in the centre, with two destroyers ahead. Abeam of her, on either side, two cruiser columns; and a destroyer screen in line ahead, outside these on either beam.

Torrens-Spence brought his Stringbag round. It was getting darker at last, now that the sun had set. Streaks of violet and grey slashed the orange of a Mediterranean sunset. Slowly the light faded… God! how slowly… He must keep patience, mustn't rush it, after all the trouble they had been to at Maleme. He smiled to himself at the memory.

They had only landed at Maleme at 1330 after the forenoon attack on the cruisers. Because *York* had been sunk, there was no communication with the fleet, so he'd sent off a Fulmar on a recce. Meanwhile he'd flown to Greece to scrounge the only torpedo in the country. They'd found two more at Maleme, but these two Swordfish were the only serviceable torpedo bombers in that part of the world. The fighter had returned at 1600 with the position, course and speed of the enemy battleship, which made the job easy.

Torrens-Spence and Kiggell were fed up with waiting.

*Look!* At last, the dusk strike from *Formidable*…! It was 1835.

Torrens-Spence counted six Albacores and two Swordfish. *Must be Saunt with 826 and 829 Squadrons. Better join up and take station astern of them…*

This was not so easy. Every time he altered course towards the approaching strike it sheered away. *We must look like CR.42 biplane fighters,* he thought. After ten minutes' hovering, both groups recognised each other and the two Maleme Swordfish joined up. The dusk strike then turned 090 degrees to the line of advance of the Italian fleet ahead of them. At 4,000 feet they hovered, biding their time while twilight faded.

Below them, the enemy ships were waiting…

# CHAPTER 16

## *Twilight End*

To Admiral Iachino it seemed an eternity since the British Fleet Air Arm had attacked in the afternoon, but in reality it was barely three hours. Time had dragged since that last, fatal attack in which the great battleship had been grievously wounded. One torpedo had struck abreast her port after propeller; the shaft had distorted and there was nothing the Chief Engineer could do about it. *Veneto*'s speed was now a miserable nineteen knots... she was staggering like a wounded bird dragging her damaged wing. There were still 400 miles to cover before reaching the safety of Taranto.

At 1600, the Admiral's mind was clearer. A Naval High Command signal had given the enemy force as one battleship, four cruisers and twelve destroyers, 170 miles to the south-east of *Veneto*. The British battleship, he knew from Intelligence, could steam no more than 20 knots. Iachino felt relieved: the enemy battle fleet could not overhaul him before nightfall. He would alter course at dark to 230 degrees, then, after an hour or two, resume the Taranto course. That would throw the enemy off the scent: the British might have despatched their destroyers for a night torpedo attack.

There was therefore only one real fear: the British Fleet Air Arm. It was those pilots who could bring about his destruction. One more torpedo hit, and he would lie stopped, a sitting duck for the British battleships that must at this moment be forging through the darkness. At all costs he must prevent another torpedo hit from the air.

It was splendid to watch these superb ships of his manoeuvring into their night disposition. He enjoyed the breeze on his face as he leant over the Admiral's bridge-rail. The *Zara, Fiume* and *Pola* were already in station. The 3rd Cruiser Division was wheeling into station: the *Trieste, Trento* and *Bolzano.* What a splendid sight they made, with the last glimmer of daylight shining on their gleaming sides!

Iachino glanced ahead. He could just see the 8th Cruiser Squadron, the *Abruzzi* and *Garibaldi,* with the 6th Destroyer Flotilla disappearing into the night. He had detached them to Brindisi.

He glanced at the clock: 1935. Once more he turned to watch the vultures wheeling five miles astern. He felt physically sick when he saw those biplanes. *Santa Maria!* There were eight of them now… Well, it was dark at last. There was no more he could do. The fleet was concentrated: it would take courage to fly through its barrage. Yet here they came…

'Open fire!'

The sudden eruption of his fleet into action snapped the tension. The screen had opened fire from astern. The cruisers were throwing up a vicious barrage… look at those tracer shells from *Bolzano* and *Trieste*!

The deck beneath him quivered. *Veneto* herself was opening up. The clatter of the machine guns deafened him; the crack of the 6-inch A.A. armament set his nerves on edge.

The screen was making smoke: great whorls of dense, black, oily particles. Then the searchlights came on, whirling and stabbing the darkness with their beams of light. It was like a festival night in Napoli, when the fireworks showered the bay…

At 3,000 yards, the formation of torpedo bombers broke up. The Admiral's spirits lifted, and he crossed himself in gratitude.

They were wheeling away now, unable to penetrate this savage curtain of fire and splash barrage.

For a moment, when the aircraft disappeared behind the smoke, there was peace in *Veneto.* The Admiral watched the cruisers continuing to fire. Slowly the tracer gained bearing, now on his port beam, now on the bow. So the enemy weren't beaten? They must be dispersing, to attack from all quarters. Yes, he was right… there was A.A. fire now from the starboard bow also, and it was creeping down the starboard side. Anyway, the searchlight defence had proved effective. The beams must have dazzled the pilots…

'Alter course back to 300 degrees, Captain,' Iachino shouted. This might upset their attack and increase the confusion.

*'Guarda! Guarda!'* The cries of the lookouts carried downwind. The torpedo bombers were coming in again.

Admiral Iachino would never forget the next eight minutes. From every quarter, through the hail of fire, aircraft suddenly burst. Holding steady for a brief moment… down on the surface… A splash, and then away, wheeling and clawing for height. In they came, all together, from different bearings. Through the smoke, past the dazzling searchlight beams, nothing could stop these gallant fliers.

Through every second of this interminable attack, Iachino was tensed for the sudden jolt of a torpedo hit. Suddenly there were no more aircraft, but machine guns were still hose-piping and tracer was still plumping into neighbouring ships. Then, as the cacophony was subsiding, there came a fresh outburst of firing from the starboard column. A lone Swordfish was gliding through the smoke, between the lines of ships. Her torpedo dropped. Her engine roared, audible even above this tumult.

Through the fire and the smoke she climbed. Pieces fell from her, then, as they watched, a great flash of orange flame spurted in the darkness abeam of *Veneto.* Iachino peered through the night. He could see nothing but a red glow pulsing in the vortex of flame and smoke. It died suddenly. Anxiously Iachino peered again into the darkness, but there were no more attacks. He must press on at his utmost speed. They had survived so far.

Admiral Iachino pursed his lips, buttoned the collar of his bridge-coat more tightly round his neck. The muscles of his jaws set in rigid lines. Better than anyone, he knew that this night of horror was yet young.

# CHAPTER 17

## *Night Action*

Off Matapan Rear Admiral (Air) was worried about this dusk strike. It should be over by now. The die was cast, but he hated telling his gallant aircrews to return to Crete. They were to land in the dark at Maleme, then refuel and fly on the next morning to join *Formidable* on passage back to Alexandria.

It was dark now. From his Admiral's bridge he could see the looming shapes of the battleships lumbering through the night. The flagship, *Warspite,* in the van; then *Barham, Valiant,* and finally *Formidable* bringing up the rear. From now on it was up to the surface ships. His boys had done their stuff: he wished only that the squadron would get through with more information. At 2008, aircraft 5 MG had reported *Attack completed. Probable hits.* Nothing more. How many of the strike aircraft had survived? Could they reach Crete safely in the darkness? Was the *Veneto* hit?

Denis Boyd felt miserably frustrated. To bumble on like this, at twenty knots, desperately trying to catch the enemy without knowing the fate of his fliers, was more than he could bear.

On the bridge of *Warspite,* Admiral Cunningham was faced with a difficult decision. Ahead of them, V.A.L.F. and his cruisers were in touch with an unknown force. Was the Commander-in-Chief justified in taking his battle fleet through an enemy screen of at least six 8-inch cruisers and eleven destroyers, with another reported force of two battleships, three cruisers and five destroyers ahead of the main force?

The enemy fleet was only 320 miles from its base; if it could make good 14 knots through the night, they would be under the umbrella of German aircraft by dawn. A.B.C.'s alternative was to work round to the north and get between the enemy fleet and Taranto. A daylight action could then take place.

The first choice was undoubtedly a risk. Night destroyer torpedo attacks were a speciality of the Italians. In ten minutes, if the fleet went after them, the Italian C.-in-C., with his torpedo-carrying cruisers and eleven destroyers, could leap out of the darkness, then wheel and fire in a matter of seconds. The clumsy British battleships turned all too slowly.

'What do you think, Staffie?'

The Staff Officer Operations was an astute officer: he had already noted the steely light in the eyes of the caged tiger.

'Though I think it a good idea to send in our destroyers, sir, the enemy are a pretty compact mass. Our destroyers might be mopped up by their 8-inch cruisers before we can get in amongst 'em.'

'Umm… and what d'ye say, Guns?'

'Well, sir, you know I want to let my guns off, but we haven't had a night firing practice for months.' He coughed as he added, 'There might be an awful potmess with our searchlights and starshell if we become involved in a night action.'

A.B.C. grunted, then turned to the Master of the Fleet (The Fleet Navigating Officer). 'What d'you think, eh?'

'I agree with the S.O.O., sir. I prefer a fleet action at dawn myself.'

The Admiral stamped off the bridge, the sparks spluttering. 'You're a pack of yellow-livered skunks,' he barked. 'I'm going to eat now, and see if my morale after supper isn't higher than yours.'

However, to Barnard, the Fleet Gunnery Officer, it was obvious that A.B.C. had already made his decision. At 2037 the Commander-in-Chief returned to the bridge. 'Flags,' he snapped. 'Make the following signal.' He dictated quickly:

*'IMMEDIATE. 14th D/F, 2nd D/F from C.-in-C.*

*Destroyer Flotillas attack enemy battle fleet with torpedoes. Estimated bearing and distance of centre of enemy battle fleet from Admiral 286 degrees, 33 miles at 2030. Enemy course and speed 295 degrees, 13 knots.'*

In silence he watched Captain Mack and his motley collection of eight destroyers work up to 28 knots. Their boiling wakes vanished ahead into the night. The C.-in-C. glanced ruefully at his remaining screen. There were only four destroyers left: *Greyhound, Griffin, Havock* and the R.A.N.'s *Stuart.* They'd be kept busy if the enemy decided to turn back with his night forces.

A.B.C. squared his shoulders as he squinted into the night. No point in fussing: he'd made his decision. Now to catch them.

At 2111, C.-in-C. was handed a signal. 'Signal, sir, from Orion,' the Flag Lieutenant reported briskly. 'Unknown ship 240 degrees, 5 miles, apparently stopped. Time of origin 2040.'

The Admiral turned to the Master of the Fleet. 'Course to steer for this position?'

The officer, a man of wisdom, was already plotting the new position: '280 degrees, sir.'

'Steer 280 degrees.'

The Commander-in-Chief strolled to the port wing of his bridge. He took off his cap to let the south-westerly breeze blow through his hair. It was one of those nights when you could almost feel the darkness. Visibility was barely two-and-a-half miles. The silence of the night was broken only by the swish of the great ship's bow wave as she steamed at 20 knots through this smooth sea with its low swell. From time to time the growl of the Quartermaster's voice from the voicepipe interrupted the silence as he repeated the orders from the Officer of the Watch.

Admiral Cunningham felt the tension mounting. Terror hung in the air tonight; something dreadful was about to happen.

Even as late as 2000, the Italian Admiral was granted one last chance to correct his appreciation of the situation. At 2000, he received a signal from Rome giving a D/F bearing of an intercepted signal: this placed the British fleet only 75 miles astern of *Veneto.* But, since the signal was an aircraft enemy report, Iachino again disregarded it, preferring to estimate that only one British battleship was at sea with an aircraft carrier. This force, he thought also, had only recently left Alexandria. His aerial reconnaissance had reported no enemy battle fleet at sea, therefore there *could* be no fleet at sea. This most recent aircraft signal, he considered, must originate from one of those Orion-class cruisers or from a destroyer.

It was a few minutes after this appreciation that Admiral Iachino learnt of the *Pola* having been torpedoed in the dusk torpedo bomber attack. Unable to discover how badly *Pola* was hurt, he was considering sending back his 1st Division of cruisers to help her. *Under Admiral Cattaneo,* he mused, the correct decision will be taken. *He will be quick and will decide immediately whether to sink Pola or to try and tow her back to Taranto. Though Cattaneo has just suggested sending back two destroyers,* Iachino argued with himself, *I consider that inadequate. If I act immediately, Cattaneo shouldn't encounter British forces, though there's always the chance he might run into those British cruisers. No. I must send the cruisers.*

'Yeoman,' he rapped. 'Make the following signal to the 1st Cruiser Division and 9th Destroyer Flotilla: *Immediate. Reverse course and proceed with utmost despatch to the assistance of Pola.*' He glanced at the clock: 2038. 'Repeat the signal to Rome,' he added.

He strolled over to the starboard wing of the bridge. Through his glasses he saw the blue signal lantern winking in the darkness from *Zara,* Admiral Cattaneo's flagship. She wheeled to starboard out of the line and disappeared into the night; the *Fiume,* her massive sister ship, followed in her wake.

Iachino's conscience felt soothed. *Pola* would receive adequate help now, particularly with the additional destroyers: the *Alfieri* in the van, the *Gioberti, Carducci* and *Oriani* bringing up the rear in line ahead. A powerful force, yes, and of some use to *Pola.*

He returned briskly to his darkened plot. The 1st Division would be clear by now. Ten minutes had elapsed since he had ordered them to break away. He crouched over the chart.

'What's my course for Cape Colonne?' he asked his Fleet Navigating Officer. 'At our present speed of 19 knots we should throw off our pursuers.'

'323 degrees,' his Staff Officer replied a minute later.

'Bring the fleet round to 323 degrees, speed 19 knots.'

*'Si, Ammiraglio.'*

In the darkness, the whole Italian fleet swung 023 degrees to starboard.

On the bridge of *Jervis* Captain Mack, leader of the 14th Destroyer Flotilla, stood poised, his feet astride, his binoculars pressed to his eyes. From long experience, he knew that the next hour could be decisive in this Mediterranean war. A.B.C. had given the destroyers — the ships so near to the Admiral's heart — their chance to prove themselves.

It was exhilarating to feel the wind blowing through one's hair. He turned to look at the destroyers that flanked and followed him: a stirring sight they made, cleaving the darkness at nearly thirty knots. Astern of him, in line ahead, were those of his own flotilla: *Janus* and the tribals, *Nubian* and *Mohawk*; six cables on his starboard beam, four of the second Destroyer Flotilla under Captain Nicholson in *Ilex,* then, in line ahead, *Hereward, Hasty, Hotspur.*

They had exercised night torpedo attacks so often in peacetime. It had always been exhilarating: tearing in on a darkened target, twisting and turning in line abreast, desperately trying to gain bearing on the enemy. Then the final moment of the 'Blue' turn, when all the 'Boats' turned together to fire their salvoes of torpedoes. The tubes trained abeam, the sudden jolt as the eight Mark VIIIs leapt over the side… then the black smoke streaming from the destroyers' funnels as they made their escape. In peacetime it was fun.

Tonight, it was true that they comprised a complete flotilla of eight destroyers; it was also true that they were doing nearly thirty knots. But this flotilla had never worked up together; and such a manoeuvre demanded long training, precise timing, team understanding. These were overworked boats, each desperately needing a boiler-clean and refit, their companies virtually exhausted from everlasting duties as maids-of-all-work to the fleet. Captain Mack himself was exhausted, but now, in the thrill of the chase, weariness had slipped from him. Though they were at Action Stations with their guns and tubes at the ready, Number One, Walter Scott, had climbed up to the Bridge from his Quarter in the After Control.

'Hullo, Number One. You'd better know what's in my mind in case we're in action shortly. Come in to the chart table.'

They dropped down to the well of the dimly lit cubbyhole and carefully spread the flapping canvas behind them to shut in the light.

'What d'you reckon is the enemy disposition, sir?' Scott asked, turning up the dimmer switch.

'Like this,' Mack explained, indicating a rough sketch. 'I intend working round the northward of the enemy. From the report of the shadowing Walrus, *Veneto*'s miles ahead and steaming at 12 knots to the north-westward. Once we've gained enough bearing, I'll divide the flotilla into two divisions: we'll run down on the so-and-sos from right ahead, on opposite courses, each division passing between the battleships and cruisers. What d'you think of that?' Mack looked up, his eyes hard in the subdued light.

Scott was silent for a moment. 'You'll be living up to A.B.C.'s ideas, sir. We'll certainly be close.'

'About 500 yards. With luck, confusion should reign supreme and they'll start firing on each other.'

'Yes, sir.'

Mack grinned beneath the red light. He slid out from under the canvas. 'But first we must *chercher nos moutons*, as the French say,' he muttered.

'Signal from *Ajax,* sir, to C.-in-C., repeated all ships,' his Yeoman bawled behind him. *'Three unknown ships by radar four miles ahead of me.'*

Captain 'D' scuttled into the chart house abaft the bridge screen. 'What d'you make of this?' he asked the Flotilla Navigating Officer. 'Surely V.A.L.F. has drawn across our bows?'

Together the two officers peered at the chart glowing above the machine, which traversed, ticking and grunting, beneath the paper.

'Reckon we must be ahead of our cruisers now, sir.'

'It must be us that *Ajax* has picked up, then?'

'Seems so, sir.'

The time was 2200. With a last look at his plot, Captain Mack returned to his bridge. He screwed up his eyes in the darkness. He must not visit the plot again; his eyes needed a long time to adjust after the light. Anything up to twenty minutes… he couldn't afford that tonight.

Time dragged. His eyes ached as he peered ahead through his binoculars. God! What he wouldn't give to have radar in his ship. He glanced at the luminous hands of his wristwatch: just 2230.

'Red one-two-o, sir,' the port lookout was yelling. 'Bright flash, sir, on the horizon.'

*But that's the bearing of our own battle fleet…*

God! What had happened?

Admiral Cunningham stood on the 'monkey island' alongside his Flag Captain, Captain Fisher. He could see better here. Since turning to 280 degrees at 2111, after receiving *Orion*'s signal of the stopped ship, he had formed his battle squadron into close order at 3 cables in line ahead: *Warspite, Valiant,* the carrier *Formidable* in the middle for safety, then *Barham* bringing up the rear. On either bow were the destroyers: *Stuart* and *Havock* a mile to starboard, *Greyhound* and *Griffin* to port.

For three-quarters of an hour the battle squadron had been plunging through the night. A miasma of disappointment and frustration had permeated the officers on the congested bridge of the flagship, *Warspite.* Once again, in spite of the Fleet Air

Arm, the enemy had slipped between their fingers. The men were tired, miserable and frustrated as once again sleep was denied them at their Action Stations in turret, director, or on searchlight platform; in engine, boiler or auxiliary rooms; at gun-mounting or lookout position.

'Bridge Office?' The tired voice of the Officer of the Watch droned over the W/T Office voicepipe. He was obviously a man disgusted by the proximity of all these staff officers invading the bridge. 'Repeat?'

There was incredulity in his voice; those who heard him felt the sudden excitement in his report: *'Valiant's radar reports echo eight to nine miles, bearing 2240, sir. Time of origin 2203.'* Then, glancing round, he shouted to his Captain, 'Target appears to be stopped, sir.'

'Alarm bearing red-one-o!' Captain Fisher commanded.

Admiral Cunningham watched 'B' turret swinging round below him. Its two fifteen-inch guns slowly elevated, trembling as they followed their director-layer pointers. 'A' turret, a blur in the darkness of the fo'c'sle, was already trained on the Alarm bearing.

'From *Valiant,* sir: Echo indicates a large ship, more than 600 feet long. Range six miles, Red-one-o, sir.'

The Admiral felt the excitement in the officer's voice. This could well be the *Veneto.* His heart lifted. He'd handle his battle squadron as he always handled his destroyer flotillas: boldly and decisively.

'Four Blue!' he snapped. He turned to watch his battle line turning together to port.

'Executive signal passed, sir!'

*Valiant* was looming out on his port quarter, at the identical moment that *Warspite* began to turn. The battle squadron was now in port quarter line, on a line of bearing of 280 degrees, each ship steering 240 degrees.

A.B.C. grinned in the darkness. He felt the disapproval of his staff: at no time in history had a squadron of battleships turned towards an unknown enemy force at night. The enemy destroyers that must be escorting the *Veneto* would run straight in with a torpedo attack. The four British destroyers would be busy. Within a few minutes, the Mediterranean fleet could be destroyed. Five minutes could lose the war for the Allies.

Cunningham was enjoying himself. Manoeuvring these monsters, with only six hundred yards between them, was not so simple as handling a destroyer flotilla…

'*Valiant*'s radar, sir. Ship bears 191 degrees, 4½ miles. Time of origin 2220.'

A.B.C. watched the turrets swing slowly round to the port bow. The two destroyers would foul the range…

'Tell *Greyhound* and *Griffin* to take station to starboard.' The Commander-in-Chief turned to watch the movement; slowly the darkened shapes of the two boats drew ahead, then crossed his bows. Why the hell were they so slow about it? He glanced at his watch: 2225.

He heard Commodore Edelsten murmuring behind him.

'Green two-o, sir, crossing from starboard to port, two large cruisers. There's a smaller cruiser ahead of them, I think.'

In silence, the Admiral peered through his glasses: two black silhouettes, led by a smaller one, were sliding across his field of vision.

'Power,' he snapped. 'What d'you make of them?'

Commander Power, a submariner and a professional on silhouettes, was intently searching: 'Two *Zara* 8-inch cruisers, sir, with a smaller one ahead.'

'Blue four-five,' the Commander-in-Chief shouted. 'I'm going on to the upper bridge.'

By the time the Commander-in-Chief had reached the upper bridge and again picked up the target through his glasses, the battle squadron was in line ahead again, on its original course of 280 degrees. The advancing cruisers were now on a parallel course, and both forces were closing rapidly.

The Commander-in-Chief stood motionless. It was up to the guns now. In a night action, he who fired first decided the issue. Impatiently he watched the turrets training on to the bearing.

The silence tautened the men's nerves. Above the hiss and swirl of the battleship through the swell, the Admiral heard only the orders from the director tower above him.

In the 15-inch D.C.T., the Director Layer sat crouched over his telescope. On the other side of the tower, his opposite number slowly turned his Trainer's handwheel. The Director Layer suddenly saw through his telescope a black shape sliding across his circle of vision. The Director Trainer must have been given the right-hand target, because the Director Layer could just see, from the left-hand corner of his eye, the stern of another ship.

'Director Layer sees the target.'

Calm, deliberate, a well-oiled machine. 'A' arcs were open now. 'A', 'B' and 'X' turrets were all bearing; their pointers were following correctly.

'Ready to open fire, sir,' the Director Layer heard the Control Officer reporting calmly. The Director Layer's fingers closed on the trigger. He was 'on' now, the hairline of his telescope level with the waterline below the bridge of the target.

'Open fire!'

*Ting! Ting! Ting!* The fire-gongs rang behind him. He waited for the battleship to roll back, then as the hairline swung across the waterline he squeezed the trigger.

Vice-Admiral Cattaneo, in *Zara,* was not unduly worried. He regarded his detachment by his Commander-in-Chief as an honour. As soon as he was clear of the fleet at 2110, Cattaneo set course of 135 degrees towards his damaged sister ship, the *Pola.* Mantio de Pisa, Captain of *Pola,* was a friend of his, but, Cattaneo had to admit, he would not have enjoyed steaming into the night like this had the British fleet been much less than a hundred and fifty miles away. Thank goodness the C.-in-C., Admiral Iachino, knew what he was doing.

At 2130, when the cooks had prepared a meal, Cattaneo allowed his Flag Captain to send the hands below for supper. After these torpedo attacks, the poor devils needed a rest. They might yet have to be up during the night.

The Vice-Admiral of the 1st Cruiser Division looked aft. In his wake he could see the towering mass of the *Fiume.* What splendid ships these cruisers were, packing a devastating punch, armoured, yet as fast as a British destroyer. *No wonder I feel confident,* he thought. *I'm commanding the finest cruiser division in the world.* But it was a dark night. Better send a destroyer on ahead…

'Tell *Alfieri* to take station ahead at three hundred metres.'

*'Si, Ammiraglio…'*

The blue flashing-lamp winked in the darkness. Then, at 2219, Cattaneo watched the lean silhouette creeping up on his starboard quarter. *Alfieri* swept by, then drew in ahead, her wake threshing white in the darkness.

The damaged *Pola* couldn't be far off now: less than five miles, probably.

'Keep a good look out,' he murmured to the officers around him. Picking up his glasses, he leant on the bridge screen. *My only danger,* he mused, *lies with their destroyers or cruisers.* Even so, the enemy ships were inferior if it came to a night action. Anyway, the action could only be a minor affair, as the use of main armaments at night was out of the question.

It was time for the ship's company to close up again at Action Stations. Supper should be finished by now. *Hullo, what's that?* Two red lights, hanging in the air: red pyrotechnics, the identification signal for the night. It must be *Pola:* de Pisa had always been hot on the efficiency of his lookouts.

'Make the reply,' Vice-Admiral Cattaneo shouted. He glanced at the chart table clock. He had always disliked the design of this clock: he must remember to tell the Chief Controller about it. The second-hand could easily be confused, just as he had nearly misread it then. Yes, that was right: twenty-seven minutes and forty seconds past ten. He heard the click of the signalman's shutter as the man began to flash the identification reply. *Pola* would be…

A steely blue flash suddenly suffused the darkness astern. A beam of blinding light pierced the night on a bearing of about Red 110. *Santa Maria!* What was this? *Pola* should be right ahead…

*'Sound the alarm!'* he screamed. *'Guarda! Guarda!'* He leapt for the alarm-gong knob and pushed it with all his might.

Terror had gripped him, for already he knew he was too late. As he leapt backwards to the binnacle, the darkness sprang aflame with a blinding orange light. Red flashes spurted on his port quarter, and then he heard the howl of approaching projectiles. His eyes were mesmerised by the spectacle of *Fiume* astern of him. There she lay, frozen in time, naked in the searchlight beam. Her sides gleamed, her sleek hull a perfection of line.

He gasped as the shells struck and suddenly she was enveloped in a sheet of flame; on the waterline, amidships, on her bridge, the explosions rent her apart. Almost in a moment she was aflame from bridge to stern. He saw her 'Y' turret flying through the air like a flaming torch. He couldn't believe his eyes. He bowed his head, paralysed with shock, unable to think.

It was at this moment that the first broadsides, fired from an invisible foe further to the right, screamed through the night towards his own flagship, the *Zara.* He could hear shells whispering and fluttering in the air as they passed over; then the ship shuddered as the first broadside struck.

Night was transformed into a tortured hell. He looked up and crossed himself. He felt her lift, tremble, then leap as the broadsides ripped her asunder. 'My men, trapped in their mess decks,' he murmured brokenly. 'My poor, beautiful *Zara…'*

He heard the roar of flames, then felt the heat as his bridge was engulfed. The Vice-Admiral was spared further agony: the next broadside lifted the whole superstructure clean over the side.

'Shift target, left! Target, first cruiser in the line.'

Lieutenant Philip Cole, Royal Navy, was Officer of the Watch in the battleship *Valiant.* For two hours he had been conning this monster, until he was thoroughly sick of the engine movements: 'Up two turns; down four turns.' These interminable manoeuvring alterations in engine revolutions were necessary to keep in station with the flagship, three cables ahead.

Cole had been appalled by *Warspite*'s first salvo. One moment the enemy cruisers had appeared, beautiful ships, sleek and powerful. The next, they were raging infernos.

'Open fire!'

*Ting! Ting! Ting!* Philip Cole stuffed his fingers in his ears. There was the crash of the guns, and *Valiant* listed to starboard from the recoil. He opened his eyes and watched their new target, the leading cruiser. She stood up like a house, grey and white under the starshell. The six-inch were pumping up the starshell for all they were worth, and now the ship's searchlights had joined in. What beautiful ships!

Then the broadsides struck…

Cole looked away, sickened. The cruiser was now receiving the concentrated fire of three British battleships, for *Barham* had joined in, after training her guns forward from the stopped ship which, in the darkness, appeared to be taking no interest.

He glanced at the clock: 2232. The massacre seemed to have lasted for an eternity already but, in reality, less than six minutes had elapsed since the first sighting. Range was now 3,000 yards — point blank.

Suddenly he noticed that the huge mass ahead of him was hauling out to starboard.

'Blue nine, sir,' he yelled above the uproar, as he saw the blue light winking from the signal bridge of *Warspite*. 'Admiral's altering now, sir.'

'Bring her round,' Captain Morgan shouted.

'Starboard fifteen,' Philip Cole shouted down the voicepipe exultantly. A.B.C. was handling his battleships like a flotilla. Cole grinned in the glare of the holocaust. This was more like it, more like the destroyer's life for which he yearned again.

'Well, Tanner, what d'you think of it?'

Rear Admiral (Air) Denis Boyd grinned as, at 2227, he hauled *Formidable* out of the line on the disengaged side on orders from the Commander-in-Chief.

'Ghastly, sir.'

'Poor devils…'

In less than one minute it had all been over. Bill had seen 'X' turret of the leading cruiser blown straight over the side, a flaming mushroom stalk. That exquisitely beautiful cruiser was now a blazing inferno. He felt physically sick.

'Look at that!' Denis Boyd shouted. Bill jerked round and saw *Griffin* fouling the range. A 6-inch salvo straddled her, fountains of water mantling her from sight. Bill's heart stopped. She must be a shambles now, destroyed by British battleships. As the shell splashes subsided, *Griffin* reappeared, unscathed but listing heavily to port as she altered course hard-over to starboard.

'Look, sir,' Bill shouted, 'those three enemy destroyers astern are turning to attack.' Bill saw the gallant little ships swing round into the mouths of the battleships' guns. Torpedoes leapt from the leader's tubes as she turned.

'EMERGENCY — BLUE NINE!'

The R/T crackled again on manoeuvring wave.

'Bring her round,' Denis Boyd shouted. 'Man, their destroyers have got guts, haven't they?'

*Formidable* started swinging away from the torpedoes as the battleships shifted their fire to the destroyers. *Poor blighters,* Bill thought, *they'll be blown out of the water.*

There was *Havock*, emerging from the smoke, miraculously afloat. Bill watched the battle fleet's destroyer screen racing in for the kill. *We're on our own now,* Bill thought. It felt somewhat lonely acting as the battle fleet's screen. Then he heard the

Admiral chuckling behind him. He was leaning over the bridge with nothing to do. He grinned at his Gunnery Officer.

'I'm not going to have these other fellows stealing *all* the thunder, Guns,' he chuckled. 'Loose off one round into the air. I want to be able to say that we've taken part in this battle!'

Just after the crack of the single round, the cheers of the bridge personnel were hushed as the searchlights of the fleet swung round to illuminate *Formidable.* The bridge officers stood rooted as the dazzling beams threw them into sharp relief. Of course there would be no mistake, but…

They held their breath, half expecting the first salvoes to fall…

The searchlights went out. Bill heard the Admiral breathe out heavily.

The fleet was working up speed now, its grisly work done, to get away from the torpedo threat. The ships drew clear on a course of 070 degrees, then reduced speed to arrive at the signalled rendezvous the next morning.

It was twenty minutes past midnight when Captain Philip Mack in *Jervis* intercepted a signal from *Havock* fifty miles to the eastward:

*c, but have expended all torpedoes. Request assistance.*

Captain D.14 swung his flotilla round to 110 degrees and increased speed to 28 knots. At last they'd contacted the enemy!

With hopes high, the eight destroyers, who had been searching in the darkness for the past four hours, raced through the night towards the horizon which had recently flared into light.

Then, at 0134, *Havock* amplified her earlier signal. *My 0020,* she signalled. *For one Veneto battleship, read one 8-inch cruiser.*

There was something like despair on *Jervis*'s bridge. What to do now? Turn back and resume the search for the Veneto or hold on and help *Havock?* Captain 'D' held on. At 0200, he sighted searchlights fine on the bow. Suddenly, right ahead, he saw the black dots of survivors' heads in the sheen on the water.

'Ship right ahead, sir.'

Thus, at 0230, the final *coup de grâce* was administered. *Jervis* fired four torpedoes at *Zara*, who was still burning. Two torpedoes struck her amidships. Seven minutes later, she split apart; rolling slowly over, she sank beneath the oily sea.

*Pick up survivors,* Captain D.14 signalled, *but do not lower boats.*

*Jervis* had picked up nine dazed survivors when Captain Mack sighted a red pyrotechnic about five miles to the eastward. 'Stop recovering survivors,' he ordered.

The destroyers hauled in their scrambling nets and worked up speed again; they were closing on the bearing of the red light when *Havock*'s silhouette loomed out of the night. An Aldis blinked from her bridge. Cruiser seems to be on an even keel, she flashed. Large numbers of survivors on her fo'c'sle and in water alongside.

*Thanks, chum,* Jervis replied. *Leave her to me.*

Ten minutes later, the black mass of a large cruiser hove in sight. As Captain 'D' stopped engines, he saw that the cruiser was low in the water. He took *Jervis* to within a cable of the mysterious vessel and, picking up a megaphone, shouted across the intervening water:

'What ship?'

Someone shouted, '*Pola*!'

At 0340, with 250 prisoners from *Pola* aboard, including her Captain, *Jervis* edged away from the *Pola,* her torpedo tubes trained on the beam. While she illuminated *Pola* with her searchlight, the flotilla leader slowly circled the dead ship.

'We've had our share,' Captain Mack grinned. 'Tell *Nubian* to finish her off.' He had made his decision. After careful thought, he'd abandoned the idea of towing her back to Alexandria; there was bound to be aerial retaliation at dawn.

The tribal closed in to 1,000 yards. Her torpedo splashed. There was a spout of flame amidships. The cruiser settled very slowly, taking her time. *Splash!* Another torpedo followed. *Pola* blew up, rolled over and sank.

# CHAPTER 18

*Dawn of Hope*

Dawn broke cold and clear. As the sun climbed above the horizon, those on *Formidable*'s bridge stood in silence. They were all alive to witness another dawn. But what of the enemy?

Since first light, *Formidable*'s reconnaissance aircraft had been reporting numbers of rafts and survivors to the south-westward. The fleet had concentrated at the appointed rendezvous at 0700. The destroyers had been despatched to pick up the survivors. At 1100 they had to abandon their work of mercy: German aircraft were diving on the small ships.

Reluctantly the destroyers drew off and the Commander-in-Chief set course for Alexandria, every H.A. gun and close-range weapon at the ready. Before withdrawing, Admiral Cunningham, chivalrous as always, directed *Formidable* to fly off an aircraft. The plane was to fly 50 miles to the north-westward and then transmit an S.O.S. on the Italian wavelength.

'Tanner, I'd like you to go too,' Denis Boyd said, turning towards Bill. 'Take the Walrus and accompany Swordfish 4Q. I don't want the hangars cluttered up — we're bound to be bombed soon.' He took Bill by the arm. 'You can land at Maleme.'

'Aye, aye, sir.'

'I shouldn't worry too much, if I were you, about the court-martial. You've done your stuff. It all depends on Kyne.'

The Admiral smiled. Bill saluted and turned quickly away.

So, at 1140 on the 29th of March 1941, a lonely Walrus listened to Swordfish 4Q transmitting its mercy S.O.S. The

Swordfish was at 1,000 feet, while below her, at 500 feet, flew the amphibian. Both aircraft were alert, their guns cocked, ready for trouble. By 1150 the transmission had been received and acknowledged by Rome radio.

The tension subsided. In the Walrus, Bill Tanner was listening to Brandy's un-melodious voice from the observer's cockpit, when he saw a message flashing from the Swordfish's cockpit:

*Are you quite happy if I go on?* the Stringbag asked.

*O.K., thanks,* the Walrus replied. *Have a pint ready for me at Maleme.*

When the Swordfish had disappeared into the haze, the two fliers were once more on their own. Bill remained at 500 feet; the sea glided beneath them, blue, green and streaked with mauve. The cockpit was warm from the sun and they began to feel drowsy.

'Look!' Brandy cried suddenly. 'Five miles on our port beam.'

Bill brought the amphibian round and flew down the bearing. The speck must be another survivor — but why up here, only forty miles from Crete?

As they lost height, Bill saw that it was a raft. There were two men in it.

'They're British!' Brandy shouted. 'Look, one of 'em is waving!'

Bill recognised the life-raft; it was one of the inflatable rubber dinghies British coastal forces carried. A mile away, streaky with oil, floated the pathetic remains of a smashed M.T.B.

'The fellow's frantic,' Bill shouted. 'Give him a wave. I'm landing alongside. Stand by for the bump.'

Two minutes later there was a tearing noise as the amphibian slicked along the surface. Streaking across the swell she subsided into the sea like an unwieldy sea cow. Bill taxied alongside the raft, and Brandy steadied it while Bill cased back the throttle until the propeller was ticking over.

'How bad is he?' Brandy shouted, pointing to the unconscious man.

The survivor shook his head. 'Pretty bad, sir. That swine of an aircraft shot us up before we knew what was happening. Out of the sun, he came…'

'What ship?' Brandy shouted.

'M.T.B. 213, sir.'

'Can you climb aboard?' Brandy yelled. 'I'll come down to lift him out.' He nodded at the unconscious man.

Bill dared not leave the cockpit, for the Walrus was bucketing in the swell. Brandy managed to drag the unhurt survivor into the amphibian, then they both grappled with the injured man. Bill could not see over the lip of the cockpit, but he heard Brandy gasping as, with the aid of a bowline, they struggled to hoist up the slumped body. There was a final heave and then Brandy yelled:

'All aboard, Bill.'

'Comfortable?'

'Yes, thanks.'

Bill opened the throttle and the Walrus took off again, leaping across the low swell. Finally she broke free of the surface and began climbing. Bill sighed with relief: she was gaining height, even with this load. Brandy was clutching the main plane above him, so conversation was impossible. The coastline of Crete came up, and twenty minutes later Bill lowered the wheels.

'Hold on, Brandy,' he instructed. Maleme was beneath them, its barren airstrip surrounded by the stone huts. He lost height, and then he was down on the deck, bumping and lurching to a standstill. He taxied across to the control, then cut the engine.

'Stretcher case,' Bill shouted towards the hut. He stood up in the cockpit and shed his Mae West. Then he turned to look down upon his wounded passenger.

The man's head was towards him, the sandy hair matted with blood. On his shoulders were the epaulettes of a Lieutenant-Commander. Bill glanced up at Brandy, who was standing above him on the main plane. The Midshipman nodded his head.

Bill climbed slowly from the aircraft and waited for the stretcher party. Three minutes later they had extricated the lacerated survivor.

By the side of Maleme airfield, in the shade beneath the main plane of a parked Swordfish, they laid him down. It was a silent group that clustered round the dying man: a damp survivor in oil-sodden clothes, two fliers and a couple of seamen. Slowly Brandy and Bill drew off their flying helmets. The eyelids of the wounded officer were flickering open. Recognition slowly dawned in the pale eyes, and then his lips moved. Bill crouched over him to hear the faint voice.

'It's you, Tanner?' the Lieutenant-Commander whispered.

'Yes, sir. You're all right now.' Bill took his hand and held it. There was a dark stain beneath Kyne's sodden shirt.

'Where am I?'

'Maleme, sir. We picked you out of the drink.'

The bewilderment in the eyes changed to understanding. 'Is that you, Bill?'

'Yes, sir,' Bill murmured.

The officer's eyes fluttered, then suddenly opened wide in a supreme effort. 'I'm sorry.'

Bill clutched the dying man's hand tightly.

'Made a mistake…' Kyne whispered, his eyes searching Tanner's face. 'Forgive… me?'

Bill barely caught the whispered words. He nodded, forcing himself to smile. 'Of course.'

A light gleamed momentarily in Kyne's eyes, then recognition faded as life ebbed slowly from him and his breathing ceased. Bill gently closed the dead man's eyelids, then walked blindly to the edge of the field where they left him alone.

'Dear God,' he said as he stared out to where purple shadows scudded across a turquoise sea. 'Dear God, don't let their sacrifice be in vain. Don't ever let us forget them.'

For a long minute he stared at sea and sky, seeing again in his memory the great ships, the aircraft, the men who would go home no more. He bowed his head for a moment in silent homage, then turned and began striding towards the huts.

# A NOTE TO THE READER

Dear Reader,

If you have enjoyed the novel enough to leave a review on **Amazon** and **Goodreads**, then we would be truly grateful.

SAPERE
BOOKS

Printed in Great Britain
by Amazon